MW01193397

Billionaire Unattainable

THE BILLIONAIRE'S OBESSION

Mason

J. S. SCOTT

Billionaire Unattainable

Cover Design by Lori Jackson

ISBN: 978-1-0910-6877-3 (Print)
ISBN: 978-1-946660-76-3 (E-Book)

Dedication

This book is dedicated to all my readers who like my atypical heroines, and my previous curvy girl stories. Thank you for asking for more. This one is for you. :)

Xoxoxoxoxo - Jan

Contents

Prologue

Laura

A Year Ago…

I knew I'd had way too much champagne and cake, but I wasn't quite sure what order I'd consumed them in.

A bunch of cake, *and then* a ton of champagne?

Or did I swill the champagne *first,* with the pound of cake as an afterthought?

Damn! I should have skipped this engagement party!

My stomach was upset, so I stepped outside to the patio to get some air.

Normally, I wasn't much of a drinker. I had a one-drink limit, and I stuck to it. Unfortunately, I had way too much on my mind today.

Breathe in.

Breathe out.

Breathe in.

Breathe out.

God, the last thing I wanted was to hurl on the patio of a multi-million-dollar penthouse owned by a powerful billionaire.

"What in the hell are you doing?" a deep, gravelly voice asked from a dark corner of the balcony.

Crap! There is somebody else on the patio!

"Breathing," I answered stiffly. The last thing I wanted was company when I was about to toss my cookies.

However, I did end up turning my head toward the *mystery voice* because watching all those fuzzy lights of the city of Seattle below me were making me slightly dizzy.

I was startled to see that the man was Mason Lawson. I almost groaned out loud.

Why did it have to be *him?* Mason's younger brother, Jett, was the host of the party, and the owner of the extravagant penthouse.

My memory was sketchy, but there was no way I could forget that I'd seen Mason…once. At a charity auction. We hadn't spoken, but that hadn't stopped me from admiring all his assets from afar.

He looked just as yummy now as he had that night.

"We breathe all the time," he grumbled. "You don't really *need* to try. And you were doing it pretty loud."

"Did I disturb you?"

"No."

"Am I bothering you?"

"No."

"Then why do you want me to stop?" I knew I sounded like a total idiot, but in my alcohol-muddled brain, it didn't matter.

"I just asked why you were breathing so hard. I didn't ask you to stop."

"I ate too much cake, and drank too much champagne. That almost never happens to me."

"Then why did it happen tonight?" he questioned, sounding displeased.

Or maybe Mason *always* sounded that way. It wasn't like I knew his normal demeanor.

It was a good question. Why *had* I drunk too much, and binged on cake? Now that I thought about it, I was pretty sure I'd scarfed down some of the pastries, too.

"I think I was trying to escape my own thoughts," I confessed because I didn't give a damn what I said to who at the moment.

"What were you thinking about?" he asked, like he was interrogating a witness to a crime.

Jesus! Was the guy always this…intense?

"I want to have a baby," I happily admitted, my mouth completely unchecked because of the alcohol. "I'm getting old, and nobody really wants me *and* a baby. Well, I'm sure *somebody* would marry me because I'm a supermodel. Okay, I'm a *plus size* model, but I do have money. Sometimes, when you make a lot of money, you're never sure why a guy wants to be with you. Do you know what I mean? And no guy has never wanted to be with *me*." I was rambling, but I couldn't seem to shut up.

He let out a bark of laughter that sounded like it was rusty, and that he didn't do it much.

"How old are you?" he demanded to know.

"Thirty-three. My biological clock is ticking, and I want to be young enough to still play with my kids. If I have *kids*. Plural. Although I'd be really happy if I just had one. But being an only child is lonely." Nobody knew that better than me.

"So how do you have a child if you don't have a man in your life?" he asked, sounding confused.

I slapped him on the arm. "Women don't need men anymore, silly. Well, not the *actual* man. But we do need a sperm donor. So I guess we kind of still need them. But I don't have to put up with one all the time. I just need his sperm."

"Are you trying to say that you want to have a test-tube baby?" he asked gruffly.

I nodded so hard that I made myself dizzy. "Yep. My egg, his sperm, and I'd never even have to meet the guy. I think it's better that way."

"Has it ever occurred to you that someday, that child is going to want to know something about his father?" His expression was grim.

"I'd love him or her enough to make up for the child not having two parents," I argued.

But yeah, I *had* thought about that, and *that* was probably the reason I'd cut loose and tried to forget about it at this party.

"You have time. You're beautiful and successful. You'll find somebody to do it the normal way," he said, his voice icy.

"Are you always this grumpy?" I asked.

"Are you always this chatty?" he shot back.

"As a matter of fact, I'm not. I think I'm just drunk. I guess I'd better get home."

"Do you know where it is?" he asked dryly.

"Of course I do. And you don't have to be so mean to me just because I want to have a kid. Women are doing it every day."

"I thought I was being nice," he said hesitantly. "I'm talking to you."

If he thinks he's being nice, I'd hate to see what his crabby moods are like.

"Well, thanks for the chat then," I said as I started to turn around to find my way back inside.

"Wait!" he commanded as he grabbed my arm. "I really wasn't trying to be mean."

I turned back to him. "It's okay. You don't know me, and I probably sound like a crazy drunk lady."

"Are you really trying to have a child?" He grilled me as hard as he had a moment before.

"I am. I've always wanted to have a family." I felt the tears well up in my eyes, but because I was hammered, I didn't even try to control them.

He put his enormous hands on my shoulders. "You'll find somebody. You can give it some more time. Hell, I'm thirty-four and I haven't even thought about having kids. Or a wife, for that matter."

"You're a man. You can father children until you die. I can't. My clock is ticking."

"It's not ticking that damn loud," he snapped.

I was beginning to think that Mason Lawson had no idea how to be nice. But he was listening.

God, he was a handsome devil. His hair was dark, but his eyes were a smoldering gray, which I found pretty damn sexy.

"It is loud." My words came out terribly slurred. "Loud enough that I'm considering going to a sperm bank. I turn thirty-four in a couple of months."

"Have you ever considered using somebody you know? Somebody who can at least give you a medical history and a background? A guy who the kid can visit when he comes of age?" His voice was still chilly, and his eyes were focused directly on my face.

"Oh, God no. I don't know any man who'd be willing to do *that*."

"I might know one," he rasped.

"Who?"

I wanted desperately to hear his answer, and I was pretty sure that he actually uttered *"Me!"* before I passed out in his arms and he caught me before I hit the ground.

Chapter 1

Laura

One Year Later…

"Are you pregnant yet?"

I rolled my eyes as I heard the graveled voice of Mason Lawson come through my cell phone. As usual, he sounded unhappy, but for him, that was his *normal* tone.

Not that I hadn't been aware of *exactly* who was calling before I'd reached for my cell phone in my home office.

It was six p.m. on a Sunday. I'd been getting the same call for the last year.

Every Sunday.

At exactly six p.m.

Mason was nothing if not reliable—right down to the second.

"I didn't go to the clinic this week, no," I informed him with a sigh, just like I did every single week. "How do you always know that I'll be home every Sunday?"

"Good," he said, acknowledging the fact that I hadn't gone to get artificially inseminated during the days prior to his weekly call.

"And I *know* that you'll be in your office on a Sunday because you're a workaholic. Since most people are doing family stuff on Sunday, and most businesses are closed, it's the best time to work in peace."

I snorted. "I guess *you* would know. You're in your office now, too, right?"

"Of course," he answered. "I'm at my most productive on Sunday."

I rolled my eyes even though he couldn't see me. Maybe I did work a lot, but I was nowhere close to being as obsessed with my business as Mason was with his.

Then again, I didn't own one of the biggest tech companies in the world, and I wasn't a billionaire.

Having the same exact call with him *every single week* really was nonsense.

The fact that I continued to answer it every time was ludicrous, too. There had to be some kind of solution to the madness.

"Can't we just like...make some kind of agreement that *if* I get inseminated, I'll let you know instead of doing this weekly thing every single Sunday?"

"No," he said gruffly.

"Why?"

"Because I feel that if I keep reminding you what a bad idea it is, it won't happen."

I sat up straight in my office chair, thumping my drawing pencil against the half-finished image in my sketchbook.

The drumming of the pencil got louder as my irritation grew.

Honestly, I was more pissed off at myself than I was with him. *Why in the hell had I been so relieved when he'd refused my solution?*

Did I really like this every Sunday torture?

"What if I don't answer my phone?" I asked grumpily.

"I'm always well-prepared to leave a detailed message," he said calmly.

Of course he is!

Mason was always prepared for *anything*. The man was like a robot who never made a wrong move.

I tossed my pencil onto my sketch pad, afraid that if I didn't, I'd injure the work I'd already done on a new design.

Over the last year, Mason and I had formed a very cautious friendship. A *casual* friendship. Oh, hell, maybe it would be more accurate to say we were *sort of* friendly acquaintances.

Mind you, Mason Lawson wasn't the type of guy to be an actual hangout buddy. I was fairly certain he didn't have the time…or the inclination…to do much that didn't include work.

He was abrupt.

He was annoying as hell.

And God, he was bossy. In fact, he was so demanding, so self-controlled and exacting, that I doubted anybody refused him *anything* unless they were family who could get away with it.

Well, I guess there was *me.*

My road to success had been so long and difficult that I wasn't about to take any shit from *any* guy. Not anymore. But Mason had been so persistent in his weekly calls that, at this point, I pretty much just ignored him and told him what he wanted to hear because it was the truth.

Maybe I'd thought that he'd finally give up and stop calling.

But he hadn't.

Really, I had to give it to him…Mason was tenacious.

I didn't hear from him at any other time except…

Six o'clock.

On Sunday.

Like freaking clockwork.

Yeah, we *ran into each other,* but I guess it was stretching things to say we were even friendly acquaintances.

Mason's younger brother, Carter, had married my best friend, Brynn, about nine months ago. So we'd been forced into each other's company a lot during their nuptials.

Now, we were only six days away from his brother Jett's wedding, and since I'd gotten close to Jett's fiancée, Ruby, Mason and I had seen each other a lot during *their* pre-wedding activities, too. I was a bridesmaid, and he was a groomsman for Jett. It was hard *not to see* Mason under the circumstances. Since Jett and Ruby had waited a long time to get married, there had been some kind of wedding activity every week for the last several weeks. Jett wanted to make sure that his bride-to-be had the full wedding experience, and I was pretty certain that the number of events he'd planned had far exceeded Ruby's expectations.

In other words, Jett had gone ape-shit crazy about giving his fiancée the wedding of her dreams, and I would have found it incredibly sweet—if it hadn't meant seeing Mason one hell of a lot over a few months' time.

Luckily, Mason was now *all out of single brothers,* and his sisters were already married and living in Colorado.

Thank God we'll bump into each other much less often once Ruby and Jett's wedding is over.

Maybe he'll stop calling me every Sunday and asking me if I'm pregnant.

I wanted to bang my head against my desk when I reminded myself exactly *why* Mason knew such sensitive information about me. Why he knew that I was considering artificial insemination. Stupidly, I'd blurted it all out to him in a drunken state at Jett and Ruby's engagement party a year ago, so maybe I *deserved* to sit through his brief, high-handed phone calls every week.

Finally, I answered tersely, "I'm nearly thirty-five. With no man dying to marry me and have children in the future, one of these days, you *are* going to get a *yes* answer when you ask if I'm going to be a mother."

I was perfectly okay with not having a man in my life, but I *did* want a child or children. Money wasn't an issue. I was completely able to give a kid or two anything they needed, and then some. My long career as a plus size model had made me financially independent, and my business of developing a line of clothing for women of all sizes was currently booming.

My new clothing line had been one of the things that had kept me from pursuing my goal of motherhood sooner.

Brynn had been an investor in Perfect Harmony almost from the beginning. She was also a handbag designer with a very successful business of her own now, but she was still the person I talked to the most when I started feeling overwhelmed with the success of Perfect Harmony.

Brynn's husband, Carter Lawson, had also invested in Perfect Harmony because he believed in my brand. Mason had followed suit—for reasons I'd never really understood—with an even bigger sum, and my clothing line had exploded when I'd moved online about ten months ago.

Because Brynn and I were both successful with modeling, we used our significant followings on social media to push our brands. But I knew that without the money invested by Carter and Mason, I wouldn't be anywhere near as successful as I was at the moment.

Even more than the money, I'd needed their *expertise*. And I'd gotten it in the form of expert advice from every top-level marketing executive who worked for Lawson Technologies, which was another significant factor in why Perfect Harmony was flying high.

My only regret was that I'd had to put being a mother on hold to handle what had become a huge, breakout company over the last ten months.

I'd had plenty of Lawson support in scaling up my business and getting the right people in place to help me once my brand had exploded. Shipping was getting streamlined from a big warehouse, and the website had finally been smoothed out after some glitches, but I was still modeling for some of my long-term clients. So my schedule had been absolutely insane.

Things were just starting to get to a manageable pace for me, and I was able to stay in my home office more to create new designs these days. There weren't nearly as many dumpster fires to put out now that everything was running smoothly.

In fact, because I wasn't nearly as frantic anymore, in the last few weeks, I'd had time to start thinking about…

"Don't do it," Mason finally answered in an ominous voice, like he'd just read my mind.

"Stop saying that," I snapped. I had *already* heeded that cautious voice in my head that laid out all the pitfalls that could occur from artificial insemination from an anonymous sperm donor. I didn't need Mason reiterating *all of them* for me every damn week.

"You know I'm right," he replied smugly.

I desperately wanted to reach through the phone and slap his handsome face. "No, I *don't know* that," I said irritably. "I think if you had your way, I'd end up eighty years old, and we'd *still* be having this conversation. Why in the hell do you care what I do with my life anyway? We hardly know each other."

It wasn't like I hadn't asked him that question every Sunday.

Mason just chose not to answer. *Every. Single. Time.*

"I don't want to see you regret your decision," he answered brusquely.

"It's *my* decision to make. Yeah, I get the fact that a child might ask about their father someday, and I wouldn't have all of the answers I'd like to have. And even if I did, the sperm donor might not be honest. I get it, but nobody's life is perfect. I really don't need you hammering the bad parts of taking that step into my head anymore."

Really, I *should* just tell him the truth, what I'd decided. I wasn't quite sure why I didn't.

Was it because it was none of his business?

Or did I just love to torment myself every single Sunday?

"Are you okay, Laura?" he asked.

"Yes. Why?" It was an odd question for Mason to ask. Our Sunday call was usually brief and regarding only one subject: my possible decision to become a mother with artificial insemination.

His query about my personal well-being was…abnormal.

"I know the online startup of Perfect Harmony got pretty crazy. You looked kind of tired at the pre-wedding party Friday night," he explained. "Is it all getting to be too much? Do you need more help?"

"No. I'm okay. You and Carter have already helped me enough. Everything is calming down. To tell you the truth, I've just started to think about the possibility of being a mom again now that I have time to breathe." Since he was actually being nice, I figured I could do the same.

I heard Mason let out an exasperated breath before he spoke, which wasn't normal for him. For the most part, he kept *everything* in check. "What I don't get is why there isn't some man taking you to bed every damn night and trying like hell to get you what you want."

I snorted. "Sorry. But Prince Charming never arrived."

"Does he *have* to be Prince Charming?" he asked huskily. "Can't he just be a regular guy?"

Mason had *never* gotten quite this candid. Not even close. He generally just reminded me not to do something I'd regret, and then hung up. I had to admit, I was surprised enough to hesitate a moment before I answered. "He could be," I confessed. "In fact, I'd really prefer it that way. The whole Prince Charming thing is a joke. I've never found anyone who just wants…*me.* And *maybe* a family. I'm a loser magnet. I'm a plus size woman who just happens to have a lot of money and a small amount of fame. As of yet, I haven't found a man who doesn't care more about those two things than the actual woman in front of him."

"Then you're looking in the wrong places," he said hoarsely. "You're a beautiful woman, Laura. Intelligent. You care about other people through your charities, so you're compassionate. What else could a guy want? There has to be a million guys who want to knock you up."

Even though my eyes were moist with tears, I had to hold back a surprised laugh. "One," I corrected. "All I've ever wanted was *one* guy."

The right one.

"What are the requirements?" he asked in a husky voice that sent a shiver down my spine.

"For what?" I frowned. I didn't know exactly what he was asking.

"To be that guy you want."

I sighed, not quite believing that Mason and I were having this conversation. "He has to be breathing."

"So I assumed," he answered dryly.

"He has to have a job and be able to hang on to it full-time. I don't care what kind of job. I don't care how much it pays. I just want somebody who has his own income, and doesn't expect me to completely support him."

"Of course."

"If he cooks or does occasional laundry and cleaning, that's a bonus," I pondered, starting to get into the game of naming off the qualities I wish I'd found in a guy I was dating a long time ago.

"What if he can afford to take those tasks away from you by hiring someone?"

I nodded, even though Mason couldn't see me. "Even better. That means he has a *really* good job that he probably loves doing."

"What else?" he prompted gruffly.

I nibbled at my bottom lip. *Did I really want to spill my guts to Mason?* There were probably a million things I could have said to appease him, but for some reason, I blurted out the truth. "He has to be attracted to me," I said in a rush, before I changed my mind.

"That would be most of the male population, married or unmarried," he scoffed.

My heart skittered. *Did Mason really believe that every guy on the planet wanted me?* "No, it isn't," I corrected. "Mason, I'm taller than most men out there. And it's not like I'm down on myself, because I'm not. I'm a realist. I'm not a tall, *slender* model. I'm a *very* tall, big-boned female with a lot of meat on my bones. I'm a bigger woman than most men really want to see in a mainstream swimming suit advertisement. People try to fat-shame me in this profession all the time. I've fought for body diversity for most of my career, but it's been an uphill battle. Men, and sometimes even women, really don't want to see me flaunting my larger body in ads that were previously dominated by very thin women. If I'm doing work for a plus size company, nobody complains. But if I start to step outside that particular niche, I get hammered by people who don't want things to change or to be more realistic."

"You're gorgeous, Laura. If any man's dick doesn't get hard every time he looks at you, he's a moron," he replied hoarsely.

I rolled my eyes. "Then there are a lot of moronic males in the world."

I tried to keep my tone light, but I was still trying to get over the shock of Mason talking about *anything* sexual. He never had before.

"Those are pretty simple requirements." He paused for a moment before he added, "Even I'd qualify to be *that* guy."

Is he kidding?

For God's sake, Mason Lawson was probably every woman's fantasy guy.

He was filthy rich.

He was powerful in the business world.

He ran one of the biggest tech companies in the world.

He was in-your-face big, bold, and handsome enough that my panties melted every time I saw him.

Sure, he was bossy, but it wasn't intimidating to *me*. It was just part of his personality that I'd learned to blow off—most of the time.

For some reason, my instinct told me that there was so much more to Mason that I almost ached to find out just how much more.

No human being could be a machine one hundred percent of the time. I knew there was a personality and emotions beneath Mason's businesslike façade.

Unfortunately, even Brynn didn't know what went on in Mason's head, and she was married to Mason's brother.

I took a deep breath. "Yes, you would definitely be a contender," I said simply, not even willing to entertain the notion that what he'd just said was anything more than a casual observation.

Men like Mason could have any woman he wanted, and they generally didn't pick a plus size woman like me.

Like I said, I was a realist.

"I'll see you Friday night," he said, his voice back to his usual matter-of-fact tone.

It was almost a relief that he'd gone back to the Mason I recognized and had grown accustomed to.

I'll see you Friday?

It took me a second to realize that I'd see him at Jett and Ruby's rehearsal dinner. "Good-night, Mason."

I waited for him to hang up.

"Good-night, Laura," he said in an unreadable tone.

The phone went dead before I realized that, for the first time, Mason had actually responded in kind by wishing me a good-night instead of just hanging up like he normally did.

I shrugged off his unusual behavior as I put my phone down on my desk and got back to work.

Chapter 2

Laura

"There was something not quite right about Mason last night," I told Brynn the next morning as we met in a new café for breakfast.

The unusual conversation I'd had with him had been bugging me since I'd hung up with him last night. Yeah, I'd tried not to think about it. It was probably a fluke. But he *had* been different, and I couldn't put a finger on why it was so damn disconcerting.

I took a bite of my veggie omelet as I watched her roll her eyes.

"Don't get me wrong," she answered wryly. "I like Mason. But when is he *ever* normal? The guy is like a machine. I'm not even sure he's human sometimes."

I put down my fork and grabbed my coffee. "Yeah, that's just it," I said thoughtfully. "He normally doesn't ask questions; he issues demands. But he was actually asking me stuff about what kind of guy I'd like to find when he called last night."

Brynn coughed like she'd momentarily choked and reached for her water glass.

Nobody even noticed that she was distressed. The restaurant wasn't terribly crowded, but it was breakfast time, so everyone was bustling around to get to work on time.

We'd seated ourselves in a quiet booth in the corner so we could chat.

"You okay?"

Brynn took a few more sips of water, and then replied, "I'm fine. Don't do that to me. Are you serious? Mason asked you *that* during your usual Sunday night call? I thought it was generally a bossy two-minute conversation."

I nodded. "It usually is. He tells me not to get artificially inseminated and hangs up. But he was different last night. He stayed on the phone a little longer and asked some bizarre questions. Well, bizarre for Mason, anyway. He never really *asks* me anything except whether or not I'm pregnant."

"What did you tell him?"

I shot her a smirk. "I said I'd like a man who worked, was breathing, and who was attracted to me."

"He wanted to make sure he was baby daddy material," Brynn said with a satisfied smile right before she dug into her own breakfast. "I've always known that he had a thing for you."

Oh, God. Let's not go there again. Brynn had been trying to convince me that Mason was hot for me for a long time. She'd been adamant, like it was really possible for something like that to happen.

"He doesn't have *a thing* for me," I denied. "He just seems to think he knows what's best for every person on the planet."

"That's not why he calls you every single Sunday. Laura, he's always been attracted to you. Why in the world is that so hard for you to believe?"

I snorted and reached for my coffee. "Mason Lawson is *not* attracted to me. He's *concerned* because his brother is married to my best friend."

Brynn wrinkled her nose, which looked adorable on her, but would have made me look like a plump rabbit. "Mason," Brynn drawled, "absolutely does not waste time on anyone he doesn't like. He calls you every single week. Granted, it's a short call, but I think he does it because he's afraid you'll end up pregnant by someone other than *him*."

My eyes flew open wide and I gaped at her. "He does *not* want to be my baby daddy," I said firmly. "Brynn, that's crazy."

"I thought you said you thought you heard him say that he did at Jett and Ruby's engagement party," Brynn argued.

"I said I thought *he might* have said it. I was hammered, Brynn. You know I don't hold my alcohol well. Honestly, I remember very little about that whole night. After a couple of days of sobriety, I knew I'd probably imagined it. God, I hate myself for every single thing I did that night. I still don't even know how I got home."

Brynn looked at me quizzically. "Mason hasn't mentioned the incident? At all?"

I shook my head. "Never. Not once. Other than the fact that he reminds me every Sunday with a phone call that he *was* listening to me ramble on while we were on that patio together—before I apparently passed out."

I shuddered. I was still mortified by my behavior that night. I'd been upset because I'd been to the fertility clinic that day and started thinking about all of the reasons why having a baby with an unknown father might be problematic.

Not to mention that the whole process had felt like something that could be done just by swiping my credit card.

It was impersonal—like any normal type of shopping transaction.

Not that I considered myself a romantic, but picking a guy to father my baby like I was buying a new dress just felt…sad to me.

And then when I'd gotten to the engagement party, I'd just felt… lonely. Not that I hadn't been happy for Jett and Ruby, but the party was an in-my-face reminder that I'd never managed to find a guy who was crazy about…me. Which was why I'd decided to resort to artificial insemination. *Alone.*

Hell, I'd never had a decent boyfriend, and I'd certainly never come close to being a bride.

"I think *Mason* took you home," Brynn replied.

"I don't," I said. "I think he would have mentioned it."

Her expression got less teasing and more serious. "He was there on the patio with you, Laura. The Lawson men might have their faults, but they'd never leave a woman defenseless. He took you home."

"Why wouldn't he mention it? *Somebody* took me home, definitely. I had to take an Uber to go get my car the next morning at Jett's place. But it wasn't Mason."

I had to keep convincing myself that my good Samaritan hadn't been Mason Lawson. If it had, it would be way too mortifying to digest.

Brynn raised a brow. "Has *anybody* else ever mentioned taking you home?"

"No."

"I rest my case. Anybody else would have mentioned it," Brynn reasoned.

Okay, I'd definitely considered that not a single friend had ever revealed the fact that they'd taken me home that night. But maybe it was somebody I hadn't really known that well. Or maybe, if it had been a friend, they hadn't wanted to embarrass me.

"I always hoped it was a female since *somebody* got me out of the dress I was wearing that night before they dumped me into my bed." Truthfully, it would have taken more than one female since I wasn't exactly a lightweight.

"Why don't you just ask Mason?" Brynn asked curiously.

It was a valid question, but I didn't really have a solid answer.

"I don't think I really want to know," I confessed with a groan. "The thought of Mason stripping my clothes off down to my underwear isn't exactly something I want to think about."

Brynn shot me a questioning look. "Laura, you did a swimsuit shoot, for God's sake. Millions of men saw it. Who cares if one more guy sees you like that? You've certainly never been shy."

Actually, Brynn was wrong. Maybe I put on a good act when I was modeling, but in my personal life, I had plenty of insecurities.

I had to push myself to be bolder, to step outside of my comfort zone. But I did it for every woman who wasn't a size zero or a size two. However, it sure as hell hadn't been easy for me.

"I don't know *those* men," I said tersely. "And you know I got fat-shamed all over social media for doing that particular assignment."

"You looked absolutely gorgeous and sexy," Brynn said, her tone defensive.

I held up a hand to stop her, so she didn't feel she needed to keep justifying my swimsuit shoot. "I'm not ashamed of it, and I'm over the social media trolls. I know I'm fit because I exercise every day, and I'm healthy. It's just kind of uncomfortable to think about some unknown guy undressing me up close and personal when I'm not even conscious."

I was being honest with Brynn. I couldn't change my genetic makeup. I was taller than most guys, and I was healthier when I had some meat on my bones. Honestly, I looked good in most of my photo shoots because it was impossible to see exactly how big I actually was in pictures.

However, I wasn't about to confess that in the flesh, I felt a bit like the Jolly Green Giant—minus the pea-colored skin.

Being a regular size model, Brynn was tall, too, but I had a couple of inches on her, and her frame was delicate, dainty. Mine…wasn't.

Brynn frowned. "I think you should ask Mason—just so you can be certain something bad didn't happen that night."

"If it did, I don't remember it. I didn't get pregnant, and I didn't contract any kind of STD." There had never been any sign of me being sexually assaulted, but I had done a visit with my doctor to make sure nothing weird had happened.

Still, there was that lost time…

It was disconcerting that I'd completely lost my memory of what had happened that night after I'd spilled my guts to Mason on the penthouse patio.

Not knowing *what* had occurred during that blacked-out time was the thing that bothered me the most.

Somebody had gotten me safely home.

Somebody had driven me in their vehicle.

Somebody had somehow gotten my substantial, limp body up to my condo.

Somebody had taken most of my clothes off, covered me up, and left my place after they'd made sure I was in bed.

It was more than a little creepy that I had no idea exactly *who* had done all that.

"Ask him," Brynn insisted. "At least you'll know."

"Maybe I will. I'll see him at the rehearsal dinner this week." The whole conversation reminded me that I really *did* need to know what happened, even if it meant that I had to ask the embarrassing questions. "Usually, our conversations are so short that I don't have the opportunity."

"Until last night, right? Things changed. What else did he say?" she prompted.

I dropped my fork on my empty plate. "He did mention that *he* fit my qualifications for what I wanted in a man. Which *doesn't* mean he wants me. I think he was just trying to say my standards weren't all that specific. I swear, he thinks every guy in the world thinks I'm irresistible."

"He'd be right," she said stubbornly as she leaned back in her bench seat and crossed her arms.

I raised my brows as I took a quick sip of coffee. "Really? Then tell me why every boyfriend I've ever had was a complete jerk."

"Because you've never demanded *more*," Brynn answered immediately. "They were selfish. None of them cared about *you*. Every one of them wanted something *you* could give *them*. Let's take Justin, for example. He was so stuck on himself that he wasn't capable of giving a damn about somebody else."

I cringed. It had been a couple of years since Justin, and I hadn't had the desire to be with another guy since. Not because my relationship had been so good with him, but because it had been so *bad*.

Brynn was right. He'd been a conceited prick. Justin had been a male model with physical perfection. But his career had never quite flourished. All he'd really wanted was my modeling contacts and my help to put him in the limelight.

"He didn't exactly have a lot of depth," I agreed.

She shook her head. "It wasn't just that. He was using you. You deserve somebody who cares about you, Laura. Sometimes I have to wonder if you don't believe, deep down, that you don't deserve anything better."

Her comment left me wondering the same thing.

My ex had never ceased to make me feel like I was *less than* because I was a plus size model, even though he wanted my help. It had pretty much been the same way with every man I'd dated, even before I'd filled out to plus size. "Hey, at least none of the losers lasted long," I said with false cheer.

Every romantic relationship I'd had in my life had been brief and far less than meaningful.

She sat up straighter and put her elbows on the table. "But you need somebody who's going to last forever. And they need to give a shit about you more than they do about themselves," she said in a serious tone.

"Prince Charming never arrived," I answered grimly, repeating what I'd told Mason the night before.

"He's definitely not Prince Charming, but I think you should give Mason a try, Laura. At least you'll know he's not after your money or your fame," Brynn cajoled. "There's *something* there. Even Carter thinks so. There's a reason Mason calls you every single week. There's a reason he looks at you like he does every time he sees you in person."

"How does he look at me?"

Brynn's expression turned into a mischievous grin. "Like he's stripping you naked in his mind."

"He's *not* attracted to me," I grumbled. I'd certainly never seen a lascivious glance from the man. "Mason Lawson is gorgeous, rich, and highly intelligent. And God knows he's driven. But he's been calling me once a week for a whole year now, Brynn. Don't you think he would have asked me out if he wanted to?"

"Not necessarily," Brynn said thoughtfully. "Carter says that Mason hasn't thought about much of anything except work for over a decade. He hasn't had a girlfriend since college. Apparently, he's probably shy and way out of practice when it comes to dating. In the dating arena, he might be unsure of himself."

I nearly spit out my coffee. I swallowed it hastily and started to laugh. "Mason? You mean the Mason who bosses everyone around? That guy?"

She grimaced. "Okay, maybe he *isn't* shy when it comes to work and running everyone else's life. But he's not a player, Laura. Carter says he never has been."

I hesitated a moment and stopped laughing before I said, "No woman would turn Mason down. He's the whole package. Well, except for his annoying habit of telling me what to do. But I think he only does that because nobody has ever really challenged him on it."

Brynn made a face. "Nobody challenges him because all he does is talk to *employees* for the most part. And you're beautiful, talented, and intelligent. No guy would refuse you, either. For God's sake, you're Laura Hastings, supermodel and successful business owner. You could have any man you wanted, too."

"Obviously, I can't find the right one," I joked. "And although I appreciate your confidence, Mason Lawson *isn't* dying to date me, so let's just drop it."

Contrary to what my best friend believed; I didn't think there were any successful, thoughtful men dying to go out with me.

Deep down, maybe I did think that I didn't deserve more than someone who used me. My self-esteem was constantly a work in progress. I'd tried so damn hard not to let my childhood rejection make me feel like I didn't deserve better, but it still got the better of me sometimes.

"We'll see," she replied ominously. "Are you bringing a date to the rehearsal dinner?"

"No."

"Then you know you're probably going to get stuck sitting by Mason, unless he brings somebody."

I felt an irritating ache in my chest at the thought of Mason showing up with a date. "Is he thinking about bringing someone?" I tried not to sound jealous. Because I wasn't. I was just…curious.

Brynn smirked. "Not that I know of. Admit it, you're attracted to him, and you don't want to see him with another woman."

I rolled my eyes. "If he did bring someone, it's none of my business."

I sounded a lot calmer than I felt. *Dammit!* Why should I give a damn if Mason wanted to drag along a dozen women to the rehearsal dinner if he wanted to?

"You'd care," Brynn said confidently.

I shot her the most nonchalant expression I could muster. "Mason and I have absolutely no future prospects of getting together as anything other than acquaintances."

"Hey, don't get defensive. It's me you're talking to," Brynn said in a slightly injured voice.

I was immediately contrite. I usually talked to her like a sister, but Mason was a tough subject for me to discuss. "Okay, honest truth," I said in a defeated tone. "I'm attracted to him. But it's definitely unrequited lust. So there's no point in even discussing him."

"Maybe there is—"

"Stop!" I warned her with an admonishing look.

Brynn laughed and winked at me, but she changed the subject.

I was grateful when she started talking about her business instead of grilling me about Mason.

It would be way too much of a stretch for me to imagine Mason's smoldering gray eyes assessing me with anything even resembling desire.

No point in even contemplating how *that* would look.

Or how I'd react if he ever did.

Chapter 3

Laura

The wedding rehearsal went off without a hitch on Friday.

The rehearsal dinner was another matter entirely.

When I arrived at the small waterfront restaurant that Jett had entirely bought out for the evening, I was surprised when I realized we weren't all sitting at one big table.

There were way too many guests for that to happen.

Flaunting tradition, Ruby and Jett had apparently invited *all* their friends and family. I mean, *why not?* Jett certainly had the space. There wasn't a single regular customer in the restaurant.

Definitely not a small, intimate dinner with just the wedding party and close family.

Not that I minded a larger crowd. I wasn't exactly shy about socializing with a lot of people. I attended plenty of events where mingling was a necessity.

I moved toward the center of the restaurant.

The venue wasn't exactly crowded, but there were plenty of guests wandering around the bar area, getting a drink before they found their table. Others were already seated.

I wandered toward the bar myself as I looked at the names next to the place settings.

"Laura!" I heard Brynn's voice call my name, and I turned around to see her waving from the other side of the room.

My best friend looked absolutely stunning in a dark-navy cocktail dress as she rushed over. Brynn always appeared to be effortlessly gorgeous, but she and I had both learned the tricks of the modeling trade, so I knew that seemingly simple beauty was actually carefully executed to look that way.

Thing was, Brynn would look fantastic even *without* makeup and in a pair of ratty sweats. *Me?* Not so much.

"You're sitting over here," she said excitedly as she took my hand and pulled me over to a small table.

I eyed the table for two suspiciously. "Do I really need to look to see who's sitting across from me?"

She beamed at me as she snatched up the card next to the second plate.

I looked at the one word printed on the paper: *Mason.*

"Brynn," I groaned. "Is this a setup?"

"Of course not," she answered, trying hard to look indignant. "It's just that you two are both solo."

I stared at her, trying to assess whether or not the whole thing was innocent.

It wasn't.

I knew Brynn almost better than I knew myself. Her gaze didn't quite meet mine. "You planned this?" I accused.

"I might have *suggested* that you two were both coming alone to Ruby."

"And *she* sat us together," I said with a sigh.

"Don't you want to sit with Mason?"

I shrugged. "I don't really mind. I just don't want to be shoved off on Mason because I'm alone. He's family. He's the brother of the groom. He should be sitting near Jett and Carter."

"Actually," a low baritone drawled behind me, "I asked Jett to make sure we were seated together, too. It wasn't just Ruby's idea."

My heart skipped a beat as I turned to see Mason standing right behind me.

It was impossible for me *not* to stare. The man looked delicious in a custom gray suit with a gray and burgundy tie.

He looked like he was accustomed to wearing a suit, but he definitely didn't look...*tame*. To me, it seemed like he really wanted to shed the confining clothing, but knew that he couldn't, and he'd accepted that fact reluctantly.

"So, you're not exactly being *shoved off on me*," he concluded.

I shot a glance at Brynn, who was slowly backing away from the whole situation.

Traitor!

"Thanks," I said as I looked up at him. "It's just...awkward."

Oddly, I *did* have to tilt my head a little to see his face, even in two-inch heels, which was a novelty for me. Mason was tall. *Really tall.* He was built like a bulldozer, with shoulders so broad that he could—and probably did—shoulder a hell of a lot of problems on top of that massive amount of space.

The guy was huge, but his body was so ripped that there didn't appear to be an extra ounce of fat on him.

He was pure muscle.

Mason's overly large presence was daunting, but not uncomfortably so; not for a woman as big as I was, anyway.

I almost felt petite standing next to him, and that was saying something.

He stepped forward and pulled out my chair. "Sit."

I bit my lip to keep from smiling. It seemed incongruous that he was being polite by pulling my chair out, yet he was barking a command at me like I was an employee.

But, I sat.

The sweetness of the gesture somehow overrode the gruff demand.

He took his place in his own seat across from me and dropped something next to my plate as he grumbled, "My application. I'm officially applying."

I stared at the manila envelope for a moment, confused. "I don't understand," I told him.

He picked up a menu and looked it over as he said calmly, "I fit your required qualifications. I have a very good job, and I'm obviously breathing since I'm speaking right now. There's no reason why I can't be your go-to guy. Granted, I'm no Prince Charming, but I'm fairly certain I can get you pregnant. I'm more than willing to try until I do."

My breath caught as I realized exactly what he was trying to convince me to think. "This is a sick joke," I said stiffly. "And I don't appreciate it."

It hurt that Mason was one of the few people in my life who knew that I wanted to have a child, and he was choosing to make a joke out of it.

"Nothing funny about it. Do I look like I'm laughing?" His eyes left the printed words on the menu and became laser-focused on me.

My body infused with an almost unbearable, incendiary heat as our gazes met. He *was* deadly serious, and from the way he was staring at me, I was starting to think he found *me* to be a more tempting dinner option than what was on the menu.

Ridiculous! Mason Lawson doesn't want me that way. It's not possible.

However, I could tell he wasn't making fun of me. He was serious.

"No. I guess it's not a joke," I said breathlessly, trying to calm my racing heartbeat. "It's just…weird."

He shrugged. "Didn't you look over a man's history, attributes, physical characteristics, education, and all that other stuff to find out if he's a suitable father for your child?"

"I did," I admitted as I reached for the glass of ice water beside my plate. I needed something to wash down the huge lump in my throat. After I swallowed, I added, "I hated it."

"Why?" he questioned in a husky tone. "It's all part of the process, right?"

I grappled with how to explain to a man like Mason exactly how I'd felt going through that process.

He was matter-of-fact. Businesslike. Unemotional. He let *reason* control his life.

He'd probably never understand how alone I'd felt in the clinic that day.

I looked down at my own menu, so I didn't have to look at him. "It felt like buying a car or something. Or placing a fast food order. I just felt like it *should* have been different. A baby is a living human being. A new life being created."

Yeah, I'd known that it would be impersonal to have a baby by an anonymous sperm donor. And I'd been okay with that. Or so I'd thought—*before* I'd gone to the clinic. But since I was doing it alone as a single woman, the whole process just lacked any kind of intimacy or joy. It hadn't felt…personal. Okay, maybe *later* it would all be worth it because I'd have my child. I could lavish all the love I had to give on that kid. However, finding a donor that way had felt so damn…lonely. Which was why I'd been depressed enough to let myself drink too much at Jett and Ruby's engagement party.

"So choose me. At least you know me," he answered. "I'm more than willing to be your Big Mac."

I nearly choked on my water as I laughed, realizing immediately that he was referring to my reference about fast food.

Mason Lawson had made a joke, even though he'd never even cracked a smile.

I watched him as he went back to scanning his menu again. Mason looked unperturbed, except for a small tic I could see along his jawline.

He's nervous. And he's totally serious. This man is actually offering to father the child I want so desperately.

For a few seconds, I let my mind wander to what it would be like to have a child with *Mason Lawson.*

Then, I shut those musings down pretty damn quickly.

I *was* more attracted to Mason than I'd ever been to a guy in my entire life. Sunday phone calls aside, I liked what I knew about him. He was definitely overbearing, but I could sense it wasn't in a malicious way.

More like an I'm-used-to-being-the-boss-and-I-don't-know-how-to-do-anything-different sort of way.

We were interrupted by the waitress who came to take our drink orders. I hadn't been planning on consuming *any* alcohol considering my history with Mason, but I asked for a glass of white wine. I was pretty sure I needed it.

He asked for a Scotch on the rocks, and we were left alone again.

I took a deep breath. "Mason, you're a billionaire. You head one of the largest companies in the world. Why in the world would you even want a child with a woman you hardly know?"

He was opening himself up to all kinds of issues. Not that I'd ever sue him for anything, but I was a little concerned that he was making himself that vulnerable on purpose.

This doesn't make sense. Mason is a consummate businessman. Why in the hell is he offering me this?

"I don't want a child with *a stranger*. I want one with *you*. We'll get to know each other better," he rumbled.

I gaped at him before I asked carefully, "How? Do you want to have a child, too? With me? That makes no sense."

He shook his head. "It makes perfect sense, Laura. You're almost thirty-five, and I'll be thirty-six soon. Both of us are totally consumed with our businesses. There's no potential love interest in sight for either of us. So I propose we make a sensible agreement."

It didn't escape my notice that he hadn't really answered the question about wanting a child himself, but I had to assume it was something he wanted as much as I did. Why else would he be offering to father a kid? My question was, why hadn't he ever mentioned it? "So you've decided you want to be my sperm donor?"

He shook his head. "Not in vitro. Not in a clinical setting. The natural way. You want everything to be more personal, and I can do that."

I swallowed hard as I realized he was willing to have sex with me. *Lots of sex*, if he was planning on getting me pregnant.

I hated myself because the prospect was so damn appealing.

I was still desperately trying to process what he was offering as I asked, "But what if you meet somebody else? What if I do?"

"Hasn't happened so far," he reasoned. "I'm not going to meet someone else. Apparently, you don't think you will either since you're planning on having an unknown man's baby. There's no Prince Charming. Remember? So why not just use me, instead?"

I was speechless.

Admittedly, I'd already resigned myself to living without a man in my life. I wasn't even looking for one anymore, and committing to motherhood would solidify my decision to be alone for a very long time. That child would be my world, so dating would be out of the question for me.

Mason Lawson is offering to give me the child I've always wanted.

Incredible.

I should be jumping *all over* that opportunity, but I couldn't.

The conversation was so surreal that I couldn't even process it, or figure out why he was offering in the first place. Was he motivated to offer because he felt sorry for me?

Nope. He hasn't become the successful man he is with a bleeding heart. He has to have some kind of ulterior motive.

Again, the only rational explanation was that he wanted a child, too.

"Not going to happen," I finally told him. "Mason, we don't even know if we'd get along. This is the first time we've actually had a real conversation. Having a kid isn't a business deal. We could end up hating each other. Fighting over an innocent child. You're right about Prince Charming not showing up. I'm not even looking for a man in my life anymore. But having a baby is a very big commitment. You could meet someone—"

"I won't," he interrupted. "I already told you that."

My head was spinning because it still seemed insane that I was even having this conversation with Mason Lawson. "It would be a disaster." I hesitated before I added, "And there was one other qualification I mentioned that I needed."

He set the menu aside and looked at me, giving me his complete attention.

My heart stuttered as I met his steely gaze.

I couldn't look away.

I couldn't breathe.

I couldn't think.

I felt completely captured. Part of me wanted to run like hell, but the rest of me had no desire to get away.

Mason lifted a brow. "You wanted a man to want you," he said huskily as his eyes devoured me whole. "I can promise you that no man will ever want you more than I do, Laura. I *completely* qualify."

Holy shit!

I swallowed hard, stunned by the depth of the desire I could see in his swirling silvery stare.

I shook my head, but it was almost impossible to force out the words, "I-I-I can't."

God, getting those two little words out was probably the hardest thing I'd ever done.

"Because *you're* not attracted to *me*?" he questioned, frowning as he asked.

My stomach was aching because I could have sworn I heard a tiny inflection of disappointment in his tone. *Or was I just imagining things?*

"No. I *am* attracted to you," I said in a rush, unwilling to let him think that I was rejecting him because of *that*.

Honestly, I wanted to strip off my clothes and crawl across the table to get him naked, too.

The desire to touch every inch of his heated, bare skin was gnawing at me, making my hands shake just a little.

I wanted to know what it would be like to be with a guy who actually wanted…me. Mason did. I could see it. His expression was unveiled, and completely carnal.

"So it isn't that you don't want me?" he asked hoarsely, his lust-filled expression making my legs weak.

I shook my head as I bit my lip. Moist heat flooded between my thighs, and I crossed my legs because it was uncomfortable. "No. Definitely not because of that."

Mason was every woman's fantasy. Hell, he was definitely my favorite wet dream. And having him offer to have an endless amount of sex with me? That was almost impossible to resist for *any* female.

Especially me.

"Good. Everything else will just work itself out," he answered, sounding satisfied.

For the very first time since I'd met him, Mason Lawson actually grinned.

His usual masculine, stern expression transformed into something far different from the grim look I was used to seeing on his handsome face.

He looked...relieved.

Happier.

Way more human than I'd ever seen him.

Again, I got the impression that there was so much more to Mason beneath the surface, a part of him that people rarely saw.

And it was at that moment, during his expression of some kind of emotion other than his usual know-it-all attitude, that I knew I was completely screwed.

Chapter 4

Laura

Interestingly enough, dinner was actually pleasant.

Mason had dropped the whole baby daddy discussion, asking me if I'd just look over his information.

I'd reluctantly agreed, and we'd moved on to other topics.

Thank God!

Not that I was planning on agreeing to his crazy suggestion, but I'd really *needed* to end that topic of conversation. *Immediately.*

The discussion couldn't go any further.

Eventually, I was going to have to set Mason straight on some things, but Jett and Ruby's rehearsal dinner wasn't the time or the place to do it.

I was finally able to relax as we moved to other getting-to-know-you topics.

Mason and I were both globe-trotters. Of course, I'd traveled extensively as a model, and he circled the planet on business, so we'd had an interesting discussion about our travels, and various cultures all over the world during the appetizers.

Over the entrees, we discovered that we were both passionate about our charities, and I'd learned that we donated, and felt fiercely troubled about a lot of the same causes.

When dessert was offered, I held up my hand to the waitress who was wheeling around the dessert cart. "Nothing for me."

"Are you kidding?" Mason asked, his brow quirked as he looked at me. "You're looking at that carrot cake like you want to have a seriously intimate relationship with it."

I smiled at him. "Oh, I *want* it. But that doesn't mean I should *have* it."

He swiped a piece of carrot cake, put it in front of me, and then took some banana cream pie for himself. "Thanks," he said to the waitress, letting her move on to the next table.

I salivated over the sweet in front of me as I said, "I can't eat that, Mason. I already had a glass of wine, and way too much food."

"You can't be full. You hardly ate," he replied firmly.

I snorted. "I ate plenty. A lot more than I usually do. I have a pretty strict diet I stick to for the most part. I already cheated tonight. Big time."

"You look beautiful. Eat your cake," he grunted.

I watched as Mason dug into his pie without a single sign of remorse.

The man obviously loved his food, and he probably needed a pretty big calorie intake to fuel a body that...large.

"I do have to fit into the clothes I model," I said, exasperated. "Sweets are wasted calories. I might be a plus size model, but that doesn't mean I can slack off. Sugar goes straight to my hips."

"Your hips look fine to me. Laura, are you trying to say you think that you're fat?" He had a very unhappy expression on his face.

"No. Not really," I answered carefully. "But there is a reason why I'm not a regular model. I can't fit into the clothes."

He shrugged. "Why can't they make the clothes fit the model instead of the other way around? Then having that piece of cake wouldn't be an issue. Hell, it's not an issue anyway. You're healthy.

You have a beautiful, statuesque body. There's no reason you need to deprive yourself."

I scowled at the offending piece of cake, but I picked up my fork. *What the hell.* Today *was* a special occasion. "The business doesn't work that way. Models need to fit the clothes. And I don't starve myself. Not anymore. I'm just...careful."

His head jerked up. "Anymore?"

I started to eat my dessert, savoring every bite. "I used to starve myself down small enough to fit into a regular model size." I had no idea why I was sharing this with Mason, but I felt comfortable doing it. It wasn't like I hadn't put my own cautionary tale out there for other women. "I was thin. Dangerously thin. But I was still getting pressured by my agent and designers to drop more weight. I was popping diet pills, and not eating enough to stay alive. Long story short, I starved myself to the point where my hair was falling out, I was passing out, and my body rebelled. I got sick."

"Why in the hell would you do that?" he asked, his nostrils flaring.

"In my industry, if you don't fit into the clothes, you don't work. Brynn and I were friends, roommates, and we were in the same situation. We had to starve to stay at an abnormally small size. One night, we were both crying in our apartment in New York because we were so damn hungry. And I was still being encouraged to lose more weight, even though I was skin and bones. I think that was the night Brynn and I both realized we were slowly killing ourselves, that what we'd been doing was so incredibly unhealthy. Both of us decided together that we weren't willing to die to be thin. Brynn was already so popular that they gave in and let her get to a healthier weight. I put on weight and went to plus size modeling."

"You were literally starving to death," he said in a graveled voice.

I nodded. "If I hadn't stopped trying to chase that size-two body, I probably would have died. Some women are just naturally thin, and they're healthy that way, but I wasn't." I took a deep breath before I continued, "I looked like a walking skeleton, and I was still being pressured to get thinner." I sighed. "There's a dark side of the modeling world. A really dark side. Brynn and I have worked our butts off since that day we reached our breaking point to try to get the industry to show some body diversity. Young women coming into the industry don't need to be caught up in that kind of hell, and it's not realistic. Only a small part of the female population is meant to be a size zero or a size two. It's a bad example to set for young females who aspire to be models someday. Modeling aside, I don't want *any* young woman feeling like they have to be model thin to attract male attention—unless she's one of the few who is healthy at that size."

"Not all men find that attractive," Mason mumbled as he finished off his pie.

I shot him a doubtful look as I swallowed another piece of cake and said, "Most do."

"I don't," he grunted as he dropped his fork on his empty dessert plate.

"Why?" I couldn't keep the word from popping out of my mouth. I was curious. Most billionaires would want very beautiful, very dainty models hanging all over them.

He dropped his napkin on all of the empty plates that he'd stacked in front of him. "I played a linebacker position in college football, Laura. In case you haven't noticed, I'm a large man. It's not comfortable for me to be with a woman I'm afraid of hurting if I put my hands on her. I'm not attracted to them."

Okay. Weird. I'd seen a lot of men Mason's size who still wanted a tiny female who made them feel invincible.

I was dying to hear more. But I didn't ask. Really, his preferences were none of my business, right?

So what if he lusted over bigger, curvier women? It wasn't like I was going to sleep with him.

No matter how appealing the thought might be.

"Don't ever starve yourself again," he said abruptly. "You don't need to, and fuck what the modeling industry wants. As long as you feel good, it doesn't matter what size clothing you wear."

My heart melted, and it felt like it trickled to a puddle on the floor at my feet.

God, it felt good to hear a guy say that to me. Granted, I was okay with who I was now most of the time, but there had never been a male who hadn't made me feel like I should strive to be smaller. Maybe because every guy I'd ever been with worked in my industry, so their mindset was the same. "I think you're the first man who's ever said that," I joked.

"Then you've been with the wrong men," he said thickly.

"Maybe I have," I said, trying to keep the conversation light, even though my heart was hammering hard inside my chest.

Our conversation felt so sensual…even though it shouldn't. It was seductive that Mason seemed to find me sexy as hell exactly the way I was.

Not once had his attention strayed from me, even though there were a lot of gorgeous women in the restaurant.

He wasn't scanning the room for *something better,* or looking around for a skinnier, more attractive woman.

Mason treated me like I was the only female in the entire place.

For me, that was incredibly heady.

In my business, I was always surrounded by women who got way more attention than I did.

But not right now.

Not here.

Not with Mason.

"I have to ask you something," I said, my voice sounding breathless.

I needed to change the subject, and I couldn't think of a better way to do it than to ask him some questions that had been burning through my mind for a long time.

He nodded sharply. "Then ask."

"What happened that night in Jett's penthouse?" I asked hesitantly. "At his engagement party. I know somebody took me home, but I don't remember much after we spoke on the patio. Did you see who took me home? The last thing I remember was telling you that I wanted to be artificially inseminated. Everything else that happened that night is a blank."

A look of surprise crossed his handsome face as he queried, "You don't remember *anything* else?"

I shook my head. "I don't think anything bad happened, but I have to know exactly what *did* happen."

He frowned. "What did you think might have happened?"

"I don't know," I confessed. "When I woke up the next morning, I couldn't remember how I got home. I never drink like that. I guess all that alcohol got to me. I was upset about my visit to the clinic that day. So I overindulged, and I paid for it. I don't even know if it was a male or female who took me home. And I was—" *Oh hell, did I really want to tell Mason?* "I was out of my dress and in my underwear." I forced the words out of my mouth. If I wanted his help, I had to admit that I'd been pretty defenseless.

"You want to know if anybody took advantage of your weakness that night?"

"I do. I feel really stupid because—"

"Don't," he said gruffly. "Nothing happened. I took you home. The party was so crowded that nobody really noticed. I carried you out of the back exit, and most of the crowd was near the front area of the penthouse."

I gaped at him. "There's a back way out? Of a penthouse?"

"Of course. People may not enter and exit that way often, but there *are* two ways out. I did my best to make sure nobody had anything to gossip about."

"How did you know where I lived?" I was still shocked that it had been Mason who had taken me home.

He shrugged his enormous shoulders. "There's something to be said for being one of the richest guys in the world. I have a good security team who can figure out where just about anybody lives."

I slumped in my chair. "Oh, God," I groaned. "I'm so sorry."

"Don't be," he insisted sharply. "Shit happens. We all occasionally do something that's not exactly wise. I'm glad I was there to get you home."

I quirked a brow at him. I highly doubted that Mason ever did *anything* out of line. Somehow, I had a hard time picturing him two sheets to the wind. He liked being in control far too much. "Then what happened?"

"Nothing. I took you home."

It didn't escape my attention that, for the first time that night, Mason didn't seem to want to look me in the eyes.

He continued, "I took off your dress. I didn't think you'd want to sleep in it."

I bit my lip to keep from groaning aloud again. *Shit!* For some reason, there was nothing creepy about Mason taking off my clothes because I was so drunk I couldn't do it myself, but I was still pretty mortified.

What in the hell had I been thinking?

Problem was, I *hadn't* thought about *anything* that evening. I'd just recklessly drank until I'd passed out. It was something I'd never done before.

"I'm sorry," I muttered quietly. "You shouldn't have had to do that. But I'm grateful that nothing bad happened."

"If I had thought that you might have assumed something bad *did* happen, I would have mentioned it before. But you were talking to me at one point after I got you home. I guess you don't remember. I thought you knew it was me."

"What did I say?" I asked cautiously, not quite sure I wanted to know what else I'd babbled on about to Mason while I was in a drunken stupor.

He hesitated for a moment before he answered, "Nothing important. I just thought you were aware of who I was, and that you were home. If I'd known that you didn't remember what happened, I would have mentioned it a long time ago."

"Did I get sick?" I questioned, alarmed that I might have done *that* in front of Mason.

"No. I made sure you were okay and asleep before I left your place. I would have stayed and helped you if you were ill."

He sounded offended that I might think he'd take off if I was sick.

"So you would have held my hair back from my face if I was worshipping the porcelain god?" I teased.

He stared at me like I had two heads as he answered, "Wouldn't anybody?"

No. Hell, no. Most men wouldn't.

Obviously, he'd never heard women talk about wanting a guy who held their hair back from their face if they were getting sick and hugging the toilet.

Personally, I had no idea what it felt like to have a man who adored me that much. Not even close.

"No. Not everyone would," I finally answered.

I gazed at him until our eyes finally met, and my heart skittered as I saw the sincerity in his stormy eyes when he said earnestly, "I would."

An ache of intense longing made me shiver, and because I couldn't handle my reactions to him anymore, I *had* to look away.

My action was a survival instinct. If I was going to get through the rest of the evening with Mason, I was going to have to keep my guard up.

As rough and businesslike as Mason usually was, there was something in the blunt way he answered my questions that moved me.

It was like he was speaking to every insecurity I had, and was determined to make them disappear like magic.

Did he know that, deep down, I craved that kind of acceptance from somebody like him?

How could he?

Honestly, I knew he was just being Mason, a guy I really hadn't known until tonight.

Brynn had been absolutely right when she'd said that Mason wasn't a player.

If he was, his undivided attention wouldn't have scared the hell out of me like it did right now.

I wanted Mason desperately. He opened the door on a yawning need that I thought I had closed a long time ago.

And my hunger had absolutely nothing to do with wanting a baby daddy.

He could hurt me. Badly!

I wasn't sure where that thought had come from, but that sudden acknowledgement made me slam that damn door closed to my darkest emotions in a hurry.

Chapter 5

Mason

"I can't believe I just got kicked out of my own place," Jett said unhappily as the two of us hung out on my patio with a drink later that night. "Thanks for putting me up tonight, Mason. Ruby says it's bad luck to see her until she walks down the aisle tomorrow."

I tossed back the rest of my beer while I wondered how in the hell Jett and Ruby could have bad luck by seeing each other before the ceremony tomorrow.

My youngest brother was so damn in love with Ruby that he'd walk through hell for her, and then he'd do it again if he didn't make her happy the first time.

"Maybe you should have just gotten married fast like Carter did with Brynn," I said.

Jett shook his head. "Ruby was so damn young when we first met. And you know her history. I didn't think she was ready. And it didn't quite kill me to wait. I'm still alive. She was living with me. But I have to admit that I'm beyond ready for her to be totally mine."

Jesus! The naked longing on Jett's face gnawed at my guts. I fucking hated anyone in my family being denied anything they wanted. And Jett *needed* Ruby. Had for a long time. Maybe waiting to marry Ruby hadn't made Jett breathe his last, but it hadn't been a picnic, either.

"The wait will all be over tomorrow. I take it you don't have any reservations?" I asked, knowing damn well that all my little brother wanted was an end to the torture of not being able to call Ruby his wife.

"None." He gave me his are-you-fucking-kidding-me look as he got up and went to the bar on the patio to grab another beer. He came back with one for both of us, and he handed me the bottle before he flopped back into his chair across from me again.

"I figured," I told him. "But I guess I had to ask. I'm the oldest."

Like Jett really needed some kind of father/son discussion before his wedding?

He didn't.

But he was still my little brother.

Jett had turned on the fire pit between us, something I'd never done because I'd never been home long enough to do it. I had to admit; it was relaxing. I could hear the water from Elliott Bay lapping against the shore since it was mere feet from the patio.

It was rare that either of my brothers stopped over at my place since I wasn't right downtown. Hell, I was hardly ever here.

Years ago, I'd wanted a house instead of a condo, right on the water.

Now, I hardly ever did anything but sleep here, and sometimes I didn't do much sleeping, either.

Jett shot me a grin. "You're not exactly old enough to be my father. And you already know I'm damn happy. After I tie the knot tomorrow, you'll be the last Lawson unmarried. Your turn, man."

I shook my head as I took the top off the glass bottle with a quick flick of my wrist. "You really think I want to hook up with *anybody* after watching you and Carter go through that kind of hell? No, thanks."

"You know, it's really not all that bad," Jett joked. "Knowing that you have a woman who is always going to love you unconditionally is actually pretty amazing once you get past all the caveman instincts of really falling in love."

I shrugged. "I'm happy for you and Carter, but I don't have time for that kind of drama. It's never even been on my radar, or something I wanted."

"I call bullshit on both of those statements," he answered. "We hired upper management and a CEO so that we all had more time after years of spending every waking moment in our offices. Lawson Technologies isn't a fledgling company anymore, Mason. It's a global giant. You need to step back and take a deep breath. Carter and I are about ready to believe you don't even get laid anymore."

"I don't. Haven't in a long time," I said irritably, before I could think better of telling my little brother anything he could torment me about later.

Jett lifted a brow. "How long?"

"Never mind," I replied hastily. It had literally been years. Quite a few of them. But that wasn't something I was going to talk to my little brother about.

"Before Ruby, there hadn't been anyone for me in a long time," Jett confessed quietly.

"You were still recovering from your injuries," I argued.

He shrugged. "That was a good excuse, I guess. But truthfully, there just wasn't anybody I wanted to be with anymore. Not until I met her."

"That didn't seem to bother Carter before he met Brynn," I grumbled.

Jett chuckled. "He was a man-whore, but I think it was getting old for him, too, although he'd probably never admit it. Look at our family, Mason. Even Dani and Harper. It's like there's just one single person in the entire world who can completely make us lose our shit when we meet them. And when we do, there's nobody else for us *except* that one person."

I grunted my agreement. "I guess that makes it impossible for everybody in our family to not be monogamous."

"I'd never cheat on Ruby. For me, it wouldn't even be possible. She's all I think about. And when I'm not having direct thoughts about her, she's there, in the back of my mind. She's part of me."

"Sounds uncomfortable," I observed drily.

"At first," he admitted. "And then, it's amazing. You should try it."

"Hell, no," I argued.

He slanted me a knowing look. "Are you really going to tell me that you don't get just a little bit obsessive over Laura? I know damn well you call her sometimes, but I don't see a relationship happening. Nothing stays secret in this family very long."

I could have disagreed with him about not having family secrets that had never been revealed, but I was more interested in what he knew about Laura. "Apparently, she's not interested," I answered, trying to sound nonchalant.

Near the end of the rehearsal dinner, Laura had been polite, but it had been like she'd shut down right in front of my eyes. She'd evaded any more personal questions, and kept things light, like we were total strangers.

"Bullshit!" he exclaimed loudly. "You're out of your mind, bro. She's interested. Have you asked her out? Did she say no?"

"Not exactly," I said reluctantly. "But I did offer to be her sperm donor, and she didn't say *yes*."

Normally, I didn't discuss my private life with my little brothers because I didn't really have one, but I was getting a little desperate to figure out why Laura was so reluctant to choose a man she knew to get her pregnant. Our arrangement made sense. At least it did to me.

She wanted a child.

I could give her one.

Problem solved.

"What?" Jett looked at me like I had two heads.

"Laura wants to have a child. She was looking into artificial insemination. I offered to knock her up. She wasn't thrilled about the whole idea," I grumbled, wishing I'd kept my mouth shut.

Now, I kind of *had* to explain myself and my actions.

I swore Jett to secrecy before I dumped the whole story about what had happened at his engagement party, and why I called Laura every week.

"Damn," he mumbled after he'd heard the entire story. "I already knew she was considering an anonymous sperm donor because she mentioned it to Ruby. But how did I *not* know you had it this bad for Laura? I knew you called her, but I had no idea it was actually a weekly thing. And how could I *not* know that you cared about her so much that you offered to help her have a child?"

"Because I never mentioned it," I said matter-of-factly. "Our phone conversations have always been brief. It's not like Laura and I have a relationship."

"But you want to," he nudged. "For fuck's sake, Mason, you offered her your sperm. What guy does that unless he's crazy about a woman? You must want a hell of a lot more than just friendship."

"I don't know what the fuck I want from her," I said, annoyed. "Except to get her gorgeous ass in my bed."

"Pretty damn badly if you offered to get her pregnant," Jett insisted. "Mason, don't screw this up. She's the one. That one woman who can make you crazy and irrational."

Jett said that like it was something I was actually supposed to *want* to happen.

Maybe he liked losing his shit over a female, but I didn't.

"I'm *never* irrational," I argued. "I simply laid out my resume and my personal information in case she decided to accept my offer. It was all very businesslike."

I frowned as Jett let out a bellowing laughter that didn't stop until he choked out, "Jesus, Mason! Seriously? Please tell me that you at least told her how you felt before you did that? And I hope to hell you took her out to a nice dinner. Maybe some flowers. Gifts of affection. Anything?"

"We were actually having dinner already at your rehearsal dinner," I said defensively.

Hell, maybe he was right. *Should I have gotten her some flowers or a gift?*

Then I reminded myself that it was a business proposition, not a romance.

But Laura had said she wanted things more personal. So maybe some romance might have been appropriate.

"I presented her with my personal portfolio at the rehearsal dinner tonight," I informed him in a disgruntled tone. "I didn't think all that other stuff was necessary."

Jett started laughing again, so hard that I wanted to reach across the fire pit and slug him to shut him up.

He snorted. "Where in the hell have you been, Mason?"

"Working," I said tersely.

"When's the last time you actually had a girlfriend?"

"College," I said in a clipped voice. "Shut the hell up and stop laughing at me."

"Bro, I'm not really laughing *at* you. But holy hell, it sounds like you've never had a real romantic interest in your life, and you have no idea how to handle how you feel about Laura. That true?"

I glared at him. "Maybe."

Truth was, Laura Hastings had completely fucked me up, and I'd been in that same pathetic state for over a year.

Not that I wanted to admit that.

Ever.

But I couldn't completely deny it anymore, either.

The woman was completely fucking with my ability to concentrate fully on Lawson Technologies. She was a distraction. A big one.

"Why in the hell haven't you just asked her out so you could spend some time together?" Jett asked, his tone astonished.

"When we first met, all she wanted was a sperm donor."

"Because she hadn't found the right guy," Jett added. "Come on, Mason, level with me. I don't know what's been happening with you, but you've tried to distance yourself from Carter and me for years. Yeah, we've physically been together a lot because of Lawson Technologies. But that's business. I'm your brother, too."

I had to stop myself from visibly flinching at Jett's last statement. Probably because it was absolutely true, *and* I could hear a thread of hurt in his tone. I *had* been distant with Carter and Jett, with good reason and deliberate intent, or so I'd thought at the time. But over the years, I'd realized that my reasons didn't matter as much as they had over a decade ago, and dropping some of those walls I'd put between me and my siblings because of something I couldn't change was long overdue.

They *were* my brothers. And I fucking missed being close to both of them, and my sisters.

So I decided to start reaching out by getting real with Jett right now.

"I wanted Laura the moment I saw her over a year ago. I'd hoped that the way I thought about her all the time was just temporary insanity, and that it would go away, but it hasn't. I don't know what the fuck is wrong with me. I haven't been nearly as focused as I used to be on Lawson Technologies, and you know our corporation is my whole goddamn life. It has been since Mom and Dad died. I don't want to want a woman this damn badly." I took a deep breath and continued. "But I can't seem to stop it from happening. I call her every damn week just because I want to hear her voice. I can't stand the thought of her getting pregnant with somebody else's kid. In fact, the thought makes me insane. Which is why I finally decided to offer her an agreement. I thought maybe it would help if I knew she wasn't going to have another guy's kid. Christ, Jett, none of this shit is normal. I've given myself a year to get over it. But I just…can't."

"You're crazy about her," Jett stated firmly. "It's not going to go away."

I glared at him. "I think I'm just crazy. *Period*. This isn't fucking *me*. I feel like some lunatic has taken over my brain, and the bastard is refusing to leave. I don't lose my head over a female. Ever."

Jett grinned. "Welcome to insanity, bro. You'll get used to it. It's not going to get any better. I'm telling you from experience. The only thing that's going to help is knowing you're committed to each other. So what did she say about your offer to father her child? You said she didn't say yes, so I assume she didn't refuse, either."

"I think she thought I was nuts," I answered. "And I wouldn't disagree with her. I don't blame her for freaking out. After the fact, I think it was probably a bad idea. I think she assumes that I'm doing it because I'm busy, and I'd like to have a child, too."

Jett nodded slowly. "Maybe. You haven't really put in an effort to get to know her. Like I said, some kind of dating relationship first would have made more sense. But it's a Lawson thing. We aren't reasonable when it comes to our women. At all. We fall so hard it's like an obsession."

"Exactly," I agreed.

"But that still doesn't explain why you haven't made a move on her."

"If she turns me down flat, I'll probably never talk to her again. I'd feel like a damn stalker if I still called her every week *after* she turns me down."

"Do you care?" Jett questioned.

"Yeah. I care. I don't want to scare the shit out of her. Hell, I scare the shit out of *myself*. But I probably wouldn't be able to stop myself from calling her anyway. I think I'm losing it."

"Do you want some brotherly advice?" he queried gently.

I hesitated for a moment before I reluctantly nodded, hating the fact that my little brother was about to give me advice. However, I needed to formulate some kind of new plan, because what I'd been doing for over a year definitely wasn't working.

"If you're going to win Laura over, you're going to have to stop treating everything like a business transaction. You're going to have to make yourself vulnerable."

Yeah, well, *that* was an idea I wasn't all that crazy about. I'd shut down that part of myself years ago. The vulnerable part. I had no idea if I could ever open that door again.

Chapter 6

Laura

I *have to tell Mason the truth.*

It was almost six p.m.

On Sunday.

And rather than waiting at home for Mason's call, I was in the offices of Lawson Technologies, entering the elevator that would take me to the top of the high-rise where I knew Mason was working.

How could I *not* know where he was? He'd called me from this location every Sunday at six p.m. for the last year.

I was clutching the envelope that he'd given me at the rehearsal dinner. I planned to give it back to him in person. I owed him that since he'd given me so much of his personal information.

One of the security guys had just entered a code to allow me up to the top floor, and I watched as the doors slid closed.

Before I'd left my condo, I guess I'd never considered the fact that getting into Mason's building on a Sunday would be as difficult as it had been. The place was as guarded as Fort Knox, so Mason was already aware that I was coming. His team downstairs had called him to get permission to let me breech the executive offices.

I slumped against the wall of the elevator, my heart racing as I felt the lift start to move.

Maybe I should have just told him on the phone. Why in the hell am I here? I could have sent his information back with a courier to make sure it was put directly into Mason's hands.

I shook my head. In my heart, I knew why. My conscience was eating me alive, and I felt guilty that I hadn't just spilled the beans earlier. Granted, the rehearsal dinner hadn't been the time of the place to have a deeply personal discussion. But I could have refused to take that information and peruse the contents.

After opening the envelope full of data on him, I'd realized how much he had trusted me with, and I hadn't liked myself for not nipping this whole thing in the bud months ago.

Jett and Ruby's wedding had been beautiful, but I'd barely seen Mason yesterday. The ceremony and reception had flown by, and as part of the wedding party, Mason and I had been so busy that we hadn't had time to really talk.

Not that I would have tried to have this conversation with him during a wedding anyway, but I hadn't even had the time to warn him that I was stopping by his office in person.

I should have just told him the truth at the rehearsal dinner instead of promising him I'd look over his personal information.

I should have confessed over one of our many Sunday phone calls during the last year.

But I hadn't.

"It would have been so much easier," I whispered to myself aloud.

However, if those phone calls ended, I would have had absolutely no connection to Mason. After some soul searching, I realized that deep down, I'd *wanted* to keep that line of communication open.

Okay. Yeah. Maybe the man made me crazy sometimes, but in his own twisted kind of way, he cared.

For some weird reason, I hadn't wanted to let that go.

It wasn't until I'd started to look at his personal information, like he'd asked me to do, that I'd gotten disgusted enough with myself to face the real reason why I hadn't been completely honest with him.

I could have told Mason to go screw himself at any time.

I could have just stopped answering his calls.

Problem was, I *liked* hearing from him every week, even if he could be totally annoying, and I hadn't wanted that to end. Even if he *was* lecturing me about what was best for me.

I'd enjoyed his attention, no matter how twisted his reasons were for calling. Probably because I'd been drawn to him by some inexplicable attraction from day one.

I had to admit that maybe somewhere in the back of my mind, I'd hoped that he might ask me to meet up with him in person. Alone. Maybe something resembling a date.

But he'd never once even come close to asking me out.

Yes, he'd claimed to be attracted to me at the rehearsal dinner, and I'd believed it at the time. It was possible that he liked me enough to get me pregnant. Problem was, I knew myself. I'd never felt quite this way about *any* guy before, and I was going to want…more. Sex just for the purpose of creating a life would leave me…empty.

So I needed to stop holding on to that stupid weekly phone call.

"That ends now," I said in a low, firm voice as my nails dug nervously into the envelope in my hand, leaving tiny crescent marks on the paper.

Brynn had been right when she'd said that I had a thing for Mason. I did. But it needed to stop. Hanging onto a weekly phone call wasn't going to magically make a guy like Mason decide that he wanted…more.

In reality, I was tormenting myself, even though I hadn't faced up to the truth until very recently.

I took a deep breath as the elevator came to a halt and the doors *whooshed* open.

The air I'd taken in suddenly left my lungs as I saw Mason's tall, bulky, gorgeous form standing right in front of the open doors.

God, he looked so damn handsome, but I was a bit taken aback to see him in a pair of jeans and a button-down white shirt.

I was right. I knew he hated wearing a suit. If he didn't, he would still be all buttoned up, even on the weekend.

Unfortunately, Mason wasn't smiling, so I was pretty sure he wasn't all that happy to see me.

It doesn't matter. I need to get on with it.

"I need to talk to you," I said, trying to gather up my resolve.

His frown deepened. "Are you okay?"

Nope. Not okay at all. But I'm going to let you think that I am.

I nodded as I stepped out of the elevator. "I'm fine. I just needed to talk in person today."

He looked relieved. "Let's go to my office."

I followed him until we reached an enormous private office. He sat down in a large chair behind his desk. I dropped the big envelope onto his desk in front of him before I sat in one of the chairs in front of his desk.

Now or never. This is my chance to come clean, and I'm taking it.

No more Sunday calls.

No more half-truths.

No more hoping that Mason might eventually ask me out.

"Did you read my information?" he asked gruffly, before I could get a single word out of my mouth.

"Some of it," I admitted. "And then I realized I couldn't continue. I'd be prying into your business for no reason at all except for a promise I made you to read it. I wasn't seriously considering your offer, Mason. I'm sorry. I guess I just wanted to end the whole discussion at the rehearsal dinner, so I agreed to take the packet and look at the contents. But I really had no intention of using you as a donor. I've already made my decision."

His head jerked up, and his eyes were suddenly searching my face. "You chose another guy?"

There was hurt in his voice, and I immediately felt even more guilty than I already had *before* I'd arrived at Lawson Technologies.

His gaze was solemn, and I wondered how a guy could look so ferocious, yet so injured at the same time.

"No. It's not that." I took a deep breath and let out a long sigh. "The truth is, I decided not to go through with the whole process. I don't think I wanted a baby for the right reasons. I think I realized that a year ago right after I visited the clinic. I didn't want a baby; I wanted someone of my own, a child to love. I guess I realized how selfish those actions would be. You were right. Someday, that kid was going to want to know where he or she came from, and who the father might be. Sperm donors are anonymous, so he or she might never know. I guess if I had a strong maternal instinct to be a mother, I could justify doing it, but that wasn't my reason. Not really. Don't get me wrong, I'd love to be a mom, but I think I'd be doing it more because I didn't want to be alone anymore."

I felt tears well up in my eyes. It hadn't been easy to admit the truth to myself, but I'd had to think about my reasons for considering artificial insemination once I'd visited the clinic, and decide whether those reasons were good enough to justify getting pregnant from the sperm of a man I'd never meet. In the end, they *weren't* rational enough for me to go through with having a biological child just so I had a kid of my own to love.

I knew my motivation was more about being alone than an overpowering maternal instinct that I couldn't ignore. Honestly, I was pretty happy with my life. My work. My friendships. I didn't *need* to be a mother. For me, my actions were completely selfish ones.

Until I'd actually gone to the clinic, I hadn't thought about how my actions and their unconventional birth might affect any child I had.

I'd grow up without parents who loved me. I had a few old memories of those years they'd been alive, but mostly, all I'd experienced was rejection. Even though I had plenty of love to give a child, I had to consider if they'd still feel rejected by not having a real father. I'd come to the conclusion that there was absolutely no reason I needed to risk it.

Mason was silent, so I continued. "I decided my motivation was completely selfish. There are so many kids in the world who need a good home. Somebody to love them. And I can do that. Eventually, I'm going to adopt from the same system I came from, Mason. I was a foster child. I know what it's like to need to feel loved. I have that to give to a child or two who really needs it. And I'd be able to relate to the problems they've faced in a broken system."

"You were a foster kid?" he asked huskily.

There was empathy in his gaze, and it almost broke me. "Most of my life," I told him. "My parents died in an accident when I was young, just like yours, and I was an only child. None of my extended family wanted me. I was around seven years old when I went into New York City foster care, and I bounced from home to home until I was seventeen. When I was a teenager, I'd already been starving myself to fit into the modeling world. But nobody really noticed since I never stayed in one place for very long. I started trying to make contacts and get modeling gigs while I was still in high school. I caught a good break before I aged out of foster care, so I was one of the lucky ones. I was at least able to make enough money to keep a roof over my head with a bunch of other roommates once I turned eighteen."

There was a tense silence in the office before Mason finally said, "Don't cry."

I raised a hand to my face, and swiped at the tears that had been pouring down my face as I spoke. "I never cry," I said in a tearful voice that actually shocked me.

Okay. I *did* cry occasionally. But I rarely let anybody see those vulnerable moments. I'd learned to keep my emotions in check a long time ago.

"Why didn't you tell me?" he asked hoarsely.

When my face was finally dry, I lowered my hands to my lap as I explained, "I didn't tell *anyone* that I'd changed my mind about having a biological child. Not even Brynn. I felt like an idiot."

"You're *not* an idiot," Mason said, defending me, which only made me want to cry again.

"But I let you keep calling me every week, thinking that I was going to do something stupid when I really wasn't. Aren't you angry about that? It was a waste of time."

He shook his head slowly. "No. And calling you was never a waste of my time. I *wanted* to call you, Laura. I wanted to know how you were doing. If I hadn't wanted to, I wouldn't have called."

I felt something flutter in my belly as I finally met his eyes. "I guess I kind of liked the fact that somebody cared that I was about to ruin my entire life. Not that having a child with a sperm donor would have *really* done that, but I guess I'll never know how it would have turned out, but I'm okay with that." I took a deep breath because I knew I was running on about nothing. I finished with the truth. "It was nice to have you show some concern every week."

Really, I'd gotten addicted to those weekly calls, even though Mason pissed me off sometimes. It was pathetic, but for a woman who had no real family and had never had a guy show a lick of protective instinct toward me, it was gratifying.

He grunted. "If I'd known that, I probably would have called you every day."

I couldn't help the way my lips curved up in a small smile. How was it that Mason always seemed to say something sweet when I felt uncomfortable? "So you forgive me for not telling you before?"

Mason shrugged. "Nothing to forgive. I was pretty much doing exactly what I wanted to do. And you really didn't owe me the truth. But you did leave me sweating over whether or not you were going to pop up pregnant with another man's baby for a whole goddamn year."

My heart skittered, leaving me almost breathless. "I'm sure you were concerned because there was some kind of family connection between us. Because Brynn is my best friend, and she's married to your brother. Actually, that's kind of sweet." Maybe I'd always hoped more would come from his calls, but I was done pretending that it might.

"The way I felt about you having someone else's baby has *never* had anything to do with family, Laura. Or about friends. I didn't want you to get pregnant from a sperm donor. It was pretty much all about *me*."

His words were blunt, and I didn't know what in the hell to say. Eventually, I murmured, "I don't understand."

His intense, broody stare made me squirm as he answered, "I think it should be fairly obvious. I offered to fuck you until you ended up pregnant with *my* child. I'm attracted to you, Laura. I always have been. That's the bottom line. If some man was going to knock you up, I wanted it to be *me*."

I was almost certain my eyes were bulging out of my head as I gaped at him. "You just wanted to...be with me? No sympathy or obligation involved?"

Everything Brynn had been trying to tell me about Mason having a thing for me suddenly came into very sharp focus.

Was he trying to say he'd wanted to...fuck me? *Really?*

"Is that so hard to believe, Laura?" he asked in a husky tone. "That I just want to get you naked for no reason other than my desire to fuck you?"

I had to open and close my mouth a couple of times before I could get the word out. "Yes."

"Why?"

"For God's sake, you're Mason Lawson, billionaire and genius leader of one of the biggest tech companies in the world. Not only are you smart and rich, but you're probably the most handsome guy I've ever seen. You could have nearly any single female on the planet. Why in the hell would you want to screw me?" I blurted out the whole truth without even thinking about it. I was too stunned to do anything else.

He shot me a small grin. "You think I'm handsome?"

I rolled my eyes. "Me, and every other woman who sees you."

He acted like he had no idea how appealing he was, which was kind of hard for me to swallow. Maybe that was just as difficult to choke down as his insistence that he wanted to get me into bed so badly that he'd called me once a week for an entire year.

Sure, he'd told me that I was beautiful, and that he was attracted to me. Maybe it was just now starting to sink in that he really meant it.

I'd blown off what Brynn had said about how she thought Mason felt.

I'd blown off the look of desire I'd thought I'd seen in his eyes Friday night.

I'd blown off the fact that he'd offered to father the biological child I'd wanted.

I'd blown off every single thing he'd done or said that might lead me to believe that he just wanted to…be with me.

All because of my own hidden insecurities.

All because I couldn't even fathom the idea that Mason found me attractive…in any way.

All because he seemed like an unreachable guy, even though I'd been attracted to him, too.

As I continued to gawk at him, I finally realized the absolute truth.

Mason Lawson *did* lust after me, and all the proof I needed was staring me in the face right now.

"Why didn't you just ask me out instead of calling on a pretense every week?" I asked.

"I wasn't sure you'd be interested. And I really didn't want to lose contact with you," he said stiffly.

Oh my Lord.

Mason had no idea how attractive he was, or how he could melt the panties off nearly any female.

In fact, he didn't seem to know that most women would kill to go out with him.

You think I'm handsome?

Hadn't he asked me that?

In reality, he hadn't wanted a stroke to his ego. Not at all. He really *had* wanted me to verify that I wanted *him*, too.

He just didn't get that most women would see him as the most desirable but unattainable guy on the planet.

My heart squeezed inside my chest as I looked at his confused face, hating myself for the fact that my fears had blinded me to *his* insecurities.

Mason Lawson wasn't a billionaire playboy. In fact, I didn't think he had all that much experience with women…at all.

It made sense, in a way. He *was* a workaholic. Did he even have time to date?

It was at that very moment that everything that had happened between Mason and me in the past came to me with very sharp clarity.

He was insecure.

I was insecure.

And we'd been dancing around each other in uncertainty because we were both attracted to each other, but neither one of us could believe the other could feel the same way.

It seemed pretty ridiculous that somebody like Mason could feel that way, but he obviously had the same thoughts about me.

As what had been happening became clearer to me, my nervousness started to fade away.

I'd nearly missed the chance to know Mason because of my fears.

I wasn't willing to let that happen again.

I needed to get out of my own way.

He stood as he asked, "Have you eaten?"

I shook my head. "No."

He was hesitant before he asked brusquely, "Do you want to go get something? I'm starving."

I had to shake myself out of my musings to realize this was my second chance. "Sure. I'm hungry." I paused for a second before I asked, "Are you asking me out on a date? I'd just like to clarify exactly what we're doing here."

I was willing to be bold to make sure we were on the same page.

"Do you want it to be a date?" he asked gruffly.

"I don't know," I replied honestly. "I think I do want it to be a date, but I need to figure out how to start all over again with you. Everything I thought before was…wrong."

"Then it's whatever the hell you want it to be for now," he answered. "Friends, a date, just two hungry people eating together. I don't really give a damn right now as long as you come with me."

He held out his hand, and I let him pull me out of my chair.

I shivered as our bodies brushed together.

Suddenly, Mason Lawson, one of the most eligible bachelors in the entire world, didn't seem all that unattainable at all.

Chapter 7

Laura

"This place is amazing," I told Mason as I took a break from feasting on Kung Pao chicken.

We'd ended up settling on Chinese because we both liked it, and he'd suggested we just take it back to his place since there was very little seating inside the small restaurant.

His home was a remodeled old mansion that sat right on the edge of the water. Not at all what I'd expected, but I was learning to stop making quick judgments when it came to Mason.

Even as I sat cross-legged on his couch in the living room, I had breathtaking Elliott Bay views. I doubted there was a space in the large house where a person *couldn't* see the water.

He reached for an eggroll and devoured it in two bites. Between us was a large coffee table full of food. When we'd first carried the mass quantity of Chinese cuisine into the house, I was certain we'd barely make a dent in the pile.

I'd been wrong.

Mason was capable of demolishing a whole lot of food, and I'd been so hungry that I'd put down my fair share as well.

"I'm not here all that often," he mused. "It's been awhile since I've seen the house while there's still any natural light," he informed me as he leaned against the back of his chair again.

In the summer, the sun didn't set until around nine o'clock, so it was still light outside. "Really? God, I think I'd love to spend every moment I had here if I owned a place like this. I think I had you pegged as the downtown penthouse type like Carter and Jett."

The home was perfect. It was serene, but still close enough to the downtown area.

"I wanted a house, but it probably would have been more convenient to be right near my offices," he answered.

I smiled. Ever since I'd realized that Mason wasn't a womanizer and had his own insecurities, he'd been so much more approachable to me.

Not that the man was exactly an open book, but he was easier to talk to.

And my heart ached to really know *him*, and not *just* the handsome, arrogant billionaire façade.

Mason had wanted me to ride with him, and we'd talked like friends on the way to get the Chinese food.

Not that he wasn't still bossy and blunt, but I could live with that. He wasn't *my* boss, so I could tell him off when he got overbearing. After all, I had dealt with him every single week on the phone when he was being an ass.

"I think it's so much nicer here," I finally answered. "Who doesn't want to be right on the water? I would love to be on the waterfront, but my budget didn't stretch quite that far. So I settled on a downtown condo."

We ate in companionable silence for a few minutes before Mason requested quietly, "Tell me about growing up in the system."

I shrugged as I reached for my soda on the coffee table. "I survived it. There isn't much more to say. I wish I could say that there was a foster family I bonded with, but there wasn't. Most of them had kids of their own to worry about. When I was younger, I just wanted a family to adopt me. By the time I hit my teens, I just wanted out."

"And you found a way to get out. Not that I agree with you starving yourself to become a model, but it's pretty admirable that you made some kind of plan for your future."

I smiled at him because he sounded so disapproving about me not eating. "I was pretty desperate just to be somebody. To prove that I could be. Back then, I didn't give a damn what I had to do to get there. By the time Brynn came into the industry, I had already been a starving model for years, and seeing her go through the same thing that I had was kind of like a wake-up call for me."

"How so?"

I thought for a moment before I spoke. "She was younger. Healthier. It was like watching my own health decline all over again. I didn't want to see her keep doing the same thing over a long period of time. Starvation plays hell with a body, and it has long-lasting effects that can never be healed. Brynn was like the sister I had never had. I cared about her. I knew we both needed to stop, even though we were both really successful at that time. I hit a wall, and I knew I either had to stop starving or I was going to die. Brynn and I made a deal with each other to try to make an impact on the industry, or get out. She outgrew the clothes when she started to eat like a healthy person should. But it was a victory when they accommodated her. My healthier weight put me into modeling plus sizes, and there was starting to be a good job market for bigger models. So I was able to transition."

He scowled. "You don't look like a plus size to me."

He sounded so indignant that I laughed. "In the modeling world, if you're a size twelve, you're plus size. I'm a sixteen now, so I'm well into the plus size category for modeling, even if the clothing industry doesn't quite see that as a plus."

"You're beautiful. You have the face of an angel. It doesn't matter what size you wear," Mason rumbled.

I snorted. "Tell that to all of the people who fat-shame me on social media. I've learned to let it roll off my back because I preach being healthy and beautiful at any size, and I truly believe what I teach.

But I have plenty of critics who don't want to see me do lingerie or swimsuit modeling."

"Fuck them. I want to see it," Mason grumbled.

He sounded so genuinely in favor of looking over my half-naked shoots that I had to bite back a smile.

"I did a swimsuit gig awhile ago. And I have a shoot in a few weeks to model lingerie for a longtime plus size clothing client. I try not to let the social media bullies get to me very much. I think it's too important for women to see a realistic model in the clothing they may want to purchase."

"I saw the swimsuit shoot," he confessed as he dropped his fork onto his empty plate.

"You did?" I asked, surprised. "How?"

"I looked for it. What red-blooded male wouldn't want to see you half naked?"

The photos were out there on the internet, still...

"I took a lot of flak for that," I informed him honestly. "My critics weren't happy. It wasn't a gig that a plus size model wouldn't usually do."

"Fuck your critics," he said gruffly. "You were sexy as hell. Most guys would be lying if they said it didn't get their dick hard."

I laughed, but Mason wasn't smiling. "I think you're the only man thinking about that. Mason, I'm a plus size model."

"You were stunning in a swimsuit, Laura."

I was stunned, and I started to blush. "I'm thick."

"Then I guess thick women get my dick hard," he scoffed. "You look pretty damn hot to me. "

There was something about the sincerity in his tone that made me want to cry.

On the surface, maybe I did appear to have my shit together, but underneath, there was still a woman who just wanted to be accepted the way that I was. I wanted a man to look at me and not want to change my appearance. At all.

The fact that Mason seemed to look at me and saw nothing except perfection was so damn foreign to me.

After years of fighting modeling agencies and designers about getting real with sizes, and going through multiple boyfriends who did nothing but critique my body, it was amazingly seductive to have a man just look at me and like what he saw.

Honestly, I wasn't quite sure how to handle a guy like Mason. Maybe I wasn't completely comfortable with his perception because I wasn't used to it, but it was pretty damn enticing.

Especially his comment about *me* getting his dick hard.

Obviously, I wasn't a virgin. But sex had never been completely comfortable for me because I'd never *felt* sexy. Maybe because the guys I'd been with in the past had never looked at me with the same lust that Mason did. I'd always known that my boyfriends would have preferred me to be smaller, more like a regular model.

Whereas Mason looked at me as though he'd like to devour every damn inch of me.

How could that *not* make me want to climb his enormous body like he was an oak tree and beg him to fuck me?

"I'm insecure sometimes," I confessed. "Most of the time, I can hide it. I really believe in what I blog about. I believe people come in all shapes and sizes, and every one of them is beautiful. I believe that the modeling world is unrealistic. A size fourteen has been the most common size for a female in the United States for years, but now some studies are saying a size sixteen is the most common average. But sometimes, I'm still that girl who starved herself to fit into a world where being super thin is everything. I still compare myself to other regular models."

"Don't," Mason said insistently. "You don't need to be *them*. Just be *you*."

He sounded grumpy that I'd try to be anything else *but myself*.

"I am me. Most of the time, anyway," I told him.

"You don't seem to have any problem giving your honest opinions on your blog."

I shot him a surprised look. "You actually read our blog? It's mostly about fashion."

"Not your blog with Brynn. Although I look at that one to keep up on anything I need to know to help with Perfect Harmony. I follow your personal blog. I read every new post. And it isn't just about fashion. It's about your perceptions of the world. I like the way you're brutally honest with yourself and your audience, even if it means saying that you were wrong about something."

Okay. I was shocked. Honestly, I did blog about how I felt in my personal blog, and what women are like around the world when I traveled. There was actually very little about fashion in it. Mostly, it was about my personal journey in life. Still... "It's more of a women's blog," I explained.

I was never less than brutally honest about myself when I wrote a post, but I didn't realize any *guy* would give a damn about a female's emotional journey.

He shrugged. "I think it's a good resource for anybody who feels like they don't completely fit into their world sometimes. I mostly read it so I can learn to understand *you*."

I laughed, but I felt a little uncomfortable that someone like Mason actually cared enough about how I felt to read my blog entries. It was flattering and disconcerting at the same time. "I'm not all that complicated."

I wanted to tell him that all I *really* wanted was to feel secure in a field where I was constantly comparing myself to women who were considered perfect in the modeling world.

When I modeled, my perceived confidence was like acting. I could put on a smiling, self-assured demeanor, but I couldn't always internalize it. My blog was like my personal struggle to get to the point where I truly *felt* self-assured all the time.

"You're complicated," he disagreed. "But wouldn't you rather be complicated and contemplative instead of just being so shallow that you never think you need to keep growing?"

I tilted my head as I studied the earnest expression on his face. "I guess I've never really thought about it that way."

"Think about it," he suggested as he stood up. "I guess I'd better get you home."

I got up and started to collect the food and plates. "Mason?" I remembered one of the things I'd meant to ask him. Something I'd read in his personal documents before I'd decided to put everything away and not look at his stuff anymore.

"Yeah?" he answered as he followed me into the kitchen with the rest of the stuff from the coffee table.

"You're a workaholic. I think everybody knows that." I hesitated.

What if I was wrong?

What if I was totally off base with my conclusions?

Before I could think about it, I just asked, "Are you trying to prove something?"

"I like to work," he muttered as he put food in the fridge. "And what would I have to prove?"

"You asked me to review your stuff, and I did. Some of it. I probably shouldn't have even looked at it since I'd already decided to foster or adopt. But I..."

"You what?" Mason asked, turning to look at me after he put his load of stuff in the fridge.

"I saw your adoption certificate in the packet, Mason," I said, every word coming out in a rush because I was afraid that I could be wrong. "Do you work as hard as you do because you're not your father's natural son?"

Chapter 8

Laura

"Okay, I managed to screw up something that I was completely enjoying. A lot," I muttered to myself as I tossed my purse onto the desk in my home office.

I'd just *had* to open my big mouth about the fact that Mason had a different natural father than the rest of his siblings.

Way to shut down all communication, Laura.

I sighed as I walked to the bedroom to put on my pajamas.

Mason's resounding *"No!"* in answer to my query about being more driven because he wasn't his dad's natural child was the only reply he'd given to my stupid question.

There had been almost zero conversation between us after that.

He'd taken me back to the parking lot of Lawson Technologies, and waited for me to get into my car and exit the parking lot, presumably to make sure I was safe. After that, I'd seen him pull out behind me. He hadn't turned off until he had to head in another direction to get to his house.

We'd gone the whole damn night in friendly conversation, getting to know each other, learning to trust each other, at least a little.

I'd told him things that I probably wouldn't have admitted to anyone except Brynn.

And then, I'd screwed the whole thing up by getting way too personal.

"I let myself get too comfortable with him," I muttered irritably as I finished changing and tossed my dirty clothes in the hamper in the master bathroom.

Not that there wasn't a whole lot of sexual tension between the two of us. Hell, that had been there *before* tonight. But over the course of the evening, something had changed. At least it had for *me.*

Since Mason never judged me, and even encouraged me in almost anything I wanted to talk about, I guess I'd let myself believe that I was okay to turn the conversation toward him.

Apparently...not.

I mean, I got it. Kind of. He obviously wasn't ready to bare his soul about something that personal.

Honestly, until I'd seen his adoption certificate, I'd never heard a word about him having a different father.

Even Brynn had never mentioned it.

Maybe because he'd been little more than a baby when his father had adopted him.

I went to my office and opened my laptop. Since I'd missed working most of the day and evening, I had some things I still needed to accomplish before I went to bed.

Forget Mason.

It's not like we were really...anything to each other. Not even friends.

Maybe we *were* attracted to each other, but that was just chemistry.

"Then why do I feel like crying?" I asked myself aloud, feeling frustrated.

A rivulet of moisture fell to my cheek, and I brushed it away, mad at myself because I was making such a big deal over watching Mason emotionally shut down right in front of my eyes in his kitchen.

The light in his gaze had eclipsed.

His face had become guarded.

It was like the door to our new, budding relationship had just... slammed shut.

And dammit, it hurt.

Even though it probably *shouldn't*.

Problem was, I'd started to really like Mason tonight. The real Mason. JusI thought I was starting to understand him. And then? *BOOM!* The guy who had been supportive of me, and challenged me to look at myself differently, had completely disappeared.

Mason Lawson, billionaire and cold-blooded businessman, had returned with a vengeance.

Honestly, I had no idea what had motivated that shutdown. Did it matter all that much to him that he didn't share DNA with the father he'd loved his entire life? Was it really all that big of a deal?

As a former child in the foster care system, I knew that sharing blood didn't really mean all that much. When my parents had died, not a single one of my blood relatives had wanted to take me on as theirs to raise.

Later, I'd found Brynn, and she was the sister I'd never had, even though we didn't share even a drop of similar DNA.

Sharing blood didn't necessarily guarantee love and emotional support from family members. I knew for a fact that it didn't, which was one of the reasons why, when I'd gotten my head together, that I'd decided that fostering and adoption was the right way to go for me. If I could just help one foster child realize that they're lovable, even though they didn't have their biological parents anymore, it would mean everything to me. I knew it would probably be much more fulfilling for me than using a sperm donor to have a child of my own, and an unknown father.

I sighed as I tried to focus on my emails. Most of them were business, so I didn't have to think much about my responses as I answered. They were pretty much routine stuff.

Until I got to an email that made me pause.

It was from Hudson Montgomery.

The Hudson Montgomery, billionaire and head of Montgomery Mining.

I wasn't exactly a watcher of the most eligible billionaires in the world, but I'd have to be living under a rock not to know who Hudson, Jax, and Cooper Montgomery were. They were in every women's magazine as the men to catch because they were rich, young, and incredibly attractive.

"What in the hell does he want with me?" I whispered aloud.

I scanned the brief missive curiously. It seemed that Hudson, the oldest Montgomery brother, wanted a business meeting to discuss Perfect Harmony.

I didn't need another investor, and I had no idea how somebody like him had even heard of my company.

I shrugged. It wouldn't hurt to meet with him because he had a lot of connections.

I sent him a list of my available times for a business lunch as he'd requested. The last thing I wanted was to rebuff anybody interested in my business, and Hudson Montgomery was way too influential to blow off.

I was wrapping up my correspondence when I heard my phone blasting Taylor Swift's "Shake It Off," my current ringtone.

After struggling to get my phone out of my purse, my heart missed a beat when I looked at my caller ID.

Mason.

"Hello," I answered cautiously.

"I'm a little late today," he said huskily. "I got distracted by a beautiful blonde and missed my regular calling time."

My heart was pounding so hard I could feel every beat. "Why are you calling now? I think you already made it perfectly clear that you weren't willing to share much information about yourself with me."

"I fucked up," he answered. "I shouldn't have shut you down like that. You caught me off guard."

"You didn't mean to put that info in the packet?" I guessed.

"No. I did. If you were going to consider me as your sperm donor, you deserved to know I'm not fully a Lawson."

He *was* fully Lawson, but obviously Mason didn't see that.

"I didn't read much of your personal stuff," I explained. "I felt bad about even breaking the seal and looking at *anything* since I was no longer in the market for a sperm donor. But the document was on the top with your birth certificate."

"My father adopted me when I was eight months old," he said in a raspy voice that made it evident the subject still wasn't easy for him to talk about. "But my parents didn't tell me the truth until I was almost finished with college. They told me that they never wanted me to feel like I wasn't one of their children. They didn't want me to feel…different. Although I understood their logic, I wish I had known earlier than that."

I ached with the pain he must have gone through once he'd found out. He had already grown up believing he was his father's natural son. I found it hard to believe that he hadn't felt a little bit…betrayed. "Did you *feel* different once you found out?"

He was silent for a moment before he answered. "Yes."

"Why?"

"Because I also discovered that my biological father was an asshole. I was the result of a sexual assault that was never reported. My mom was really young. Barely eighteen. She and my bio father met by chance at some party when she was living in San Diego. Mom was drugged and assaulted by him at that party. When she ended up pregnant, not a single one of her relatives or friends believed that she had been assaulted. My bio father's family was too rich and powerful to take on, so she had no support. Luckily, she got offered a decent job in Colorado, so she moved to get a fresh start. That's where she met my father. My dad was quite a bit older than she was, but they fell in love anyway. The rest is history. My father started the paperwork to adopt me soon after I was born. The two of them were already married by then."

I let out a shaky breath. "I'm sure your father loved you, Mason. Just as much as if you were his natural son. And I doubt it changed your relationship with your brothers and sisters, either, right?"

There was a long pause before he said, "They don't know the truth. You're the only one who knows. I'd appreciate it if you didn't share it."

Oh, dear God. "You never told your siblings?"

"My parents and I planned to do it together over the holidays the year they died. They never made it to Christmas. They were killed in an auto accident right at the holidays. There was no way I was going to dump more on any of my siblings after our parents were killed."

I understood what he was saying. The timing hadn't been right, and they had all been struggling with the sudden death of their parents.

"And after that?" It had been many years since his parents had died. Certainly there had been opportunities for him to share this with his siblings.

"For a couple of years, I couldn't do it because they were still mourning our parents. Then, all of us drifted apart. We dealt with their passing in different ways. After so many years had passed, it really didn't seem to matter. My brothers and sisters have been through a lot. It never seemed like a good time to lay something like that on them."

Oh, *it mattered,* but probably not to Carter, Jett, Harper, or Dani.

It mattered to *Mason.*

A lot.

Now that I knew the truth, I realized his behavior was very similar to what I'd suggested to him at his house, and maybe I'd hit a nerve that had caused him to shut down. Mason worked to prove he *deserved* to be a Lawson because he wasn't one by blood. Sure, the siblings were all still blood-related through their mother, so they were half siblings. But obviously Mason *still* seemed motivated to show that he was willing to work harder than anybody else to have the right to claim the Lawson name.

Didn't he realize he didn't have to prove a single damn thing? He was his father's son. Period. And I knew Jett and Carter well enough to safely say that they wouldn't give a damn if Mason wasn't related by blood at all. He'd still be their brother. Nothing would change that bond between them.

My heart ached for the young man who had abruptly learned that he didn't have his father's blood flowing through his veins. At that age, and with no warning, he must have been completely devastated.

Add the fact that Mason's real father had been a rapist, and it wasn't hard to figure out why he worked so damn hard to prove that he was worthy.

"Do you think your father loved you any less because he wasn't your natural father?" I ventured carefully.

"No," he said huskily. "I know he didn't. He still considered me his firstborn son. He was there with Mom when I was born."

"Then why are you still trying to prove that you're worthy, Mason? You've sacrificed everything else in your life to turn Lawson Technologies into a world leader. *You've* done that."

"My brothers worked hard, too," he argued.

"I don't doubt that," I told him. "But they've all found a life outside of Lawson now that it's successful. Carter and Jett both mentioned that you hired upper management and a CEO a couple of years ago so you could all stop busting your asses and practically living in the office."

"We did," he answered in a clipped tone. "And you should talk. You're a workaholic, too."

I could hear the defensiveness in his voice, but I wasn't backing down. This was way too important to just let Mason slide.

"I am," I confessed. "But only to a certain point. I don't sacrifice my relationships with my friends for work. My workaholic tendencies come from a place of wanting financial security. You know my history. Plus, I love what I do. Sometimes I get really caught up in my designs because it's my passion."

Mason's motivation was far different than mine. He still felt like he *had* to work every minute of the day. So he'd lived, eaten, and breathed Lawson Technologies since his parents had died.

The guy was driven by his own demons, and he wasn't going to stop until… "You should tell them, Mason."

"Why bother at this point?" he rasped. "Do you think they deserve to know I'm not really a Lawson?"

"That's bullshit, and you know it," I said firmly. "You *are* a Lawson. You always have been. You don't owe *them* the truth. You owe *yourself* the freedom of telling them the truth. You need to see that they aren't going to give a damn what DNA you have."

I held my breath until he finally grumbled, "I'll think about it."

I had to be happy with that, because I got the sense that he wasn't ready to tell his siblings the truth quite yet. "Do you have any other siblings on your biological father's side?"

"No. The bastard died a year after I was born. Overdosed on drugs. If he hadn't, I would have killed him for what he did to my mother."

I felt my eyes well up with tears. It was so obvious that Mason had adored both of his parents. So much so that he was still trying to please them long after their deaths.

"They'd be so proud of you and what you've done with Lawson Technologies," I said honestly. "But they'd want you to be happy, too. I'll never tell anyone, Mason. That's your secret to share. Not mine. You'll do it when you're ready."

"I believe you," he replied. It was a moment before he added, "Are you going to forgive me for being a dick to you earlier?"

I sighed. It obviously wasn't easy for Mason to communicate on a personal level. Probably because he'd done a damn good job of isolating himself from everybody he cared about for so long by being a reclusive workaholic.

Truthfully, I'd *already* forgiven him, but I wasn't letting him off the hook that easily. "Weird," I said contemplatively. "I must have missed the whole apology thing."

"You want me to say it?" he asked grumpily.

"Yes. You hurt me."

"I'm sorry," he said without hesitation, like he wanted to take away any injury he'd caused me as quickly as possible. "The last thing I'd ever want to do is hurt you, Laura."

He sounded so sincere that I had to swallow a lump in my throat.

I was startled when a tear actually plopped onto my cheek and started to travel downward. I wiped it away as I realized I was actually crying. *Again. What in the hell was wrong with me?* "Forgiven," I said, trying to hide the fact that Mason touched me on a level I didn't completely understand.

I felt him so hard that I swore he could reach into my body and tear out my soul when he was hurting over something.

It wasn't that I could see or hear that he was damaged. He was a master at covering up his emotions. But for some reason, I could *feel* it. I was connected to Mason in a way that I didn't completely understand.

"Have dinner with me tomorrow." His statement was *almost* a question, but not quite. It was pretty much a command.

I smiled. "Are you asking me out? Because if you are, your technique could use some work."

"I don't *have* a technique," he said gutturally. "And yeah, I was asking you out, but I'm not taking no for an answer. I'll pick you up around seven?"

"So you are flexible on time? But not my yes or no answer?"

"Pretty much," he confessed in a gruff tone. "Just put me out of my fucking misery and say yes."

He was being high-handed, but I hadn't missed the small note of desperation in his voice that made me instantly say, "Yes. Seven o'clock is fine."

Chapter 9

Mason

Laura Hastings Blog Entry, Today, 9 a.m.

Have you ever asked a question that you thought was coming from a good place, but you wished like hell that you could take it back after you asked it?

I did. Yesterday. Although it worked out okay in the end, I guess I really need to learn that just because I'm ready to ask the question and be supportive, it doesn't mean that person is ripe to answer. Not because they're lying or trying to hide anything, but because they just haven't found the answers yet themselves.

I was immediately hurt because that person shut down when I asked something personal, because I was only trying to help. I crawled inside myself to lick my own wounds, not realizing that there was no hurt intended.

In reality, I injured him by asking too much, too soon.

I should have gotten to know him a little better before asking something really personal. And no, I'm not about to tell you all what I asked. :) I'm just hoping you can learn from my stupid mistake.

Have fun. Laugh. Make some good memories before you get too heavy with that new man in your life. Make sure that person has the chance to trust you before you distance them by rushing into something you shouldn't.

Lesson learned for me.

Smile in the mirror at yourself at least once today. You're beautiful, whether you know it or not.

Xoxoxo ~ Laura

It didn't take a rocket scientist to know that Laura was referring to what had happened between us the night before in her blog post.

I slammed my hand down on my desk after reading her blog entry for the second time that day. I'd initially looked at it this morning when I'd first checked my email.

I'd just brought up the post again, trying to figure out how I could make up for the fact that I'd just shut her down without thinking about how that might make her feel.

It wasn't that I didn't trust her. I just hadn't wanted to talk about...*that*.

"Fuck!" I cursed as I leaned back in my office chair.

I didn't want Laura to feel like she couldn't say what she wanted to say. I didn't want her to think I didn't trust her.

It wasn't *her*.

It was *me*.

I didn't actually trust *anyone* all that much. If you trusted somebody in the business world without having anything in writing, that made you a complete moron.

Laura isn't business. My relationship with her was personal, which was really the root of the entire problem.

Regardless of the advice I'd gotten from Jett, I still didn't know a damn thing about romancing a female.

I was a ruthless bastard in business.

I didn't hesitate to do whatever it took for the sake of Lawson Technologies.

My entire life was my business.

I hadn't even thought much about any particular female. Until her…

If I actually had a choice, I'd *still* be buried in Lawson Technologies every minute of the day. But ever since I'd seen Laura, and started to read her blog posts, I'd been intrigued. That curiosity had now reached a point of obsession, and I had no fucking idea how to handle *that*. Or *her*.

It wasn't like I hadn't tried for an entire year to get over my fascination with Laura Hastings. Now, I knew that wasn't going to happen.

Jett's advice had been pretty simple: *Get your mind off Lawson and focus on Laura. Care about how she feels and what she wants. And then let her know who you are.*

I scowled at the blog post again, and realized I'd been an epic fail when I'd shut her down last night.

She thought she'd tried to get close to me too soon, when in reality, I wanted her to get just as close to me as she possibly could.

Of course, my desires to be close to her included being naked, hot and sweaty.

But I also had an intense desire to make her happy, to see her smile.

So what in the hell did I need to do about *that?*

And the gnawing pain in my gut to make her mine?

I was pretty sure I was completely fucked.

As much as I'd followed her blog and gleaned certain information about the kind of woman Laura was, I still had no idea what she wanted in a man.

Which was why I'd straight out asked her.

He has to be breathing. He has to have a good job. And he has to want…me.

Hell, I'd met every one of those qualifications from day one.

There had to be…more.

Sure, I'd been relieved when she'd admitted that our attraction went both ways, but I wasn't just attracted to Laura.

I was fucking obsessed.

Maybe if I can get her beautiful ass in my bed and fuck her until we're both satisfied, my life can go back to the way it was before I met her.

There was that hope that I could somehow make it back onto the sanity train once my need to possess her had been appeased.

Honestly, I had no idea what would happen if I could actually get what I'd wanted for over a year now.

The intercom on my desk buzzed, interrupting my train of thought. "Mr. Lawson, your sister is on the line," my secretary said in her usual, professional voice.

"Thanks. I got it," I told her as I picked up the phone.

"Mason, I know you're probably busy," my sister Dani said hesitantly. "But Harper and I are leaving tomorrow, and I hoped you and Carter could meet us for lunch."

Now that Jett and Ruby's wedding was over, and the newlyweds had left for their European honeymoon, Dani and Harper were leaving to get back to their lives in Colorado.

I could tell by the tone of her voice that my sister absolutely expected me to refuse. I always did. So why should she suppose she'd get a different answer today?

I hesitated as I thought about what Laura had said the night before.

It was all true. I *had* isolated myself from my family as much as possible because I was afraid they'd look at me differently if they knew I wasn't one hundred percent their sibling. Not to mention the fact that my biological father was a sexual predator.

Problem was, I'd been so busy avoiding my own possible rejection that I hadn't once considered what kind of emotional pain it would cause for my siblings.

However, I *could* recognize how much my distance had hurt them *now.* Harper and Dani were two of the strongest women I knew, and I'd think the same thing even if they weren't my sisters.

Now that I was really listening, I could hear the inflection of sadness in Dani's voice.

I'd done that.

And I fucking hated myself for it.

"Have you already called Carter?" I asked. I was done being a dick to my own sisters.

"Not yet," she answered. "But you know Carter. He's always up for anything to bring us together these days."

Yeah, he was. After years of feeling responsible for Mom and Dad's deaths simply because they were running an errand for him when the accident had occurred, Carter was moving on, and trying to bring everyone back together in the process. In some way, every one of us had isolated ourselves for various reasons. But Carter wanted his family close again. It was like a personal mission for him.

Finally, I told Dani, "I'll go drag him out of his office and bring him with me. Where are we meeting? I'm starving. So no damn girlie food."

"You're really coming with Carter?" Dani replied, sounding stunned.

I felt like an asshole as I realized how happily surprised my sister appeared to be. Almost like she didn't believe me.

"I missed breakfast today. And I'd like to see you and Harper before you go." Strangely, I realized how true that statement actually was. For the most part, with Dani and Harper living in Colorado with their families, I didn't get to see them all that often.

"You really *want* to see us?" Dani asked hesitantly.

Holy shit! Way to make a guy feel like an asshole.

Then again, I probably deserved it.

"Carter and I will be there. When and where?" I took a quick look at my watch.

"Obviously, somewhere that they serve large portions if you and Carter are hungry," she teased.

"Definitely," I affirmed. I wasn't a salad type of guy.

We made our plans to meet around one o'clock at a café and deli known for making man-sized sandwiches.

Once I'd disconnected with Dani, I dialed Carter's number.

"Lunch," I said, getting right to the point.

"What?" Carter answered.

"Lunch," I repeated. "Meet me in the lobby in five minutes. We're meeting Harper and Dani. They have to leave tomorrow. Don't you want to see them before they go?"

Stupid question. Of course Carter wants to see our younger sisters before they left for Colorado.

"You're actually leaving the office for a family lunch?"

It annoyed me that he sounded so surprised. "Yes."

"Since when?" he asked drily.

"Since today," I grumbled. "Just get your ass to the lobby."

I swore I heard my brother chuckle as I hung up the phone.

Chapter 10

Mason

"Damn, you were chatty today," Carter observed as he flopped into the chair across from my desk after lunch. "I don't think you've ever asked Dani and Harper as many questions in an entire decade as you did today."

I sat down behind my desk as I answered, "I'm interested in their lives in Colorado. What's wrong with that?"

Carter shrugged. "Nothing. But it's not normal for you. I know you keep an eye on both of them…from a distance. But you were asking them questions *directly* at lunch today. It's just not like you."

"You said your goal was to get all of us close again, like we were when we were younger," I reminded him.

He grinned. "I didn't think you were really listening."

Jesus Christ! Carter made me sound like a dick. *Was I really that bad?* "I was listening," I said, feeling defensive. "I was just…busy."

"You're always too damn busy," Carter replied drily. "When in the hell are you going to slow it down, Mason? That was the agreement when we hired upper management and a CEO. All three of us were going to get a life. Well, I guess Jett already had one, but you and I were going to do it together. And as of now, I don't see you out enjoying your life. For Christ's sake, if I didn't know better, I'd think you had an apartment here in the building. Do you ever see your house?"

I took a deep breath before I answered, "As a matter of fact, yes. Yesterday. I was out of the office before dark."

"Yesterday was Sunday," Carter retorted. "You shouldn't have been here *at all.* No offense, man, but you're killing yourself, and it's time to sit back and enjoy the fruits of your labor. We all still work hard. But we don't have to work *that* damn hard anymore."

"I'm working on it," I grumbled, knowing Carter was right.

I *had* agreed to pass everyday management to skilled leaders and a CEO. But I'd mostly done it so my brothers could take it a little easier.

Honestly, I'd *never* really planned on doing it myself.

"Do you think you're irreplaceable?" Carter said with more than a little snark.

I glared at him, but I didn't answer. Did I think Lawson Technologies would falter if I was out of the office more? Not really. That probably wasn't why I was driven to be here all the time.

Obviously, the company still needed me, Carter, and Jett at the helm, but…

"You were the one who told me that the company wasn't going to fall apart if I took time off," Carter said in a calmer tone. "When I wanted to go away with Brynn because she needed me, and we needed to get away, you encouraged me to go without feeling guilty."

"And your point is?" I questioned.

"My point is that I want to see your stubborn ass out of the office for at least a week. More if you can handle it. I'm thinking you might end up having withdrawals. But we made a deal."

"I just…agreed. There was no deal. I wanted you and Jett to take some time off. You've already spent enough of your adult life cooped up in your offices."

Carter crossed his arms over his chest obstinately, which I knew was never a good sign.

I had a different relationship with Carter than I did with Jett. You could say it was more…confrontational. Maybe because we were closer in age.

"Yeah. Well. That's bullshit. We *all* needed some time off," Carter replied sharply. "You just haven't taken yours…yet."

"Don't need it," I snapped at him.

"I don't give a damn whether you *think* you need it or not. If you show up here tomorrow morning, your office is going to be locked. So take a week and catch up on whatever you *haven't* been doing for the last decade," Carter suggested.

Now I was pissed off. "You aren't locking up my office."

"Try coming in and you'll find out that I have done it. I talked to Jett earlier today on the phone. We're two-thirds of this partnership, and we both agree that it's time to play the 'majority rules' card."

I looked at him, dumbfounded. "You'd do that to me?"

"Shit! Don't look at me that way, Mason. We're doing this because we care. We aren't just *business partners*. We're your goddamn brothers. If you keep on living your life this way, you're going to kill yourself." He paused before he added, "You could spent some time with Laura. It's pretty obvious to me that you'd like to get to know her better. I'm not blind, brother."

"I'd like to get her into my bed," I corrected.

Carter shot me a shit-eating grin. "Then make it last a week. You'll come back to the office smiling."

"We're having dinner tonight," I admitted reluctantly. "Dinner isn't going to last a week. What in the hell am I going to do if I don't work?"

"Yeah, I used to wonder about that, too," Carter shared. "But you'll eventually figure out that there's more to life than work."

"I doubt that," I replied. "But it seems as if I don't have a choice since you and Jett have decided to gang up against me."

Damn, it hurt that my two brothers were conspiring to kick me out of my offices.

"This isn't a damn takeover, Mason," Carter said hoarsely. "It's two brothers worrying about whether you're going to make it to your fortieth birthday. Don't tell me you wouldn't do the same damn thing if you were worried about the well-being of me or Jett."

Problem was, I *couldn't* really tell Carter that.

Maybe I hadn't been the most attentive brother because I'd been so busy trying to prove that I was worthy of being a Lawson. However, I'd be perfectly willing to die to keep any one of my siblings safe.

Did I get that this entire scheme was coming from a place of concern? *Yes.*

Did I have to like it? *No.*

"I suppose I'd feel the same way," I finally answered noncommittally. "But you have to understand that I like to work."

Carter raised a brow. "No, you don't. I've always believed you've been driven to work as hard as you do. I've just never known exactly *why.*"

"Dammit! I want to make Lawson a household name," I said, frustrated.

"Done," Carter retorted. "It's a brand that's already known worldwide. We've already *made it,* Mason, just in case you missed that. Time to take a vacation. Take Laura along with you. You'll never miss any of us."

"I won't miss *you,* anyway," I grunted, irritated that I was going to have to be idle for an entire week.

Carter grinned at me, completely unfazed. "I think you really need to get laid."

"Why do you keep saying that?"

"Because it's true, isn't it?" Carter was a little more serious.

I seethed for a minute before I answered. "No!" And then I said, "Okay. Probably. But I'm not like you, Carter. I can't just charm some woman into bed in one night."

He chuckled. "My whoring days are over. The only woman I want to get close to is Brynn."

"But you used to be able to screw any woman you wanted," I reminded him.

"I did. Before I met Brynn. Once I saw her, I didn't want anyone else, and never will."

"I kind of feel the same way about Laura," I admitted. "I *can't* just go find a woman to have sex with, even if I wanted to do it, which I don't. It *has* to be her."

"Feeling a little bit obsessed?" Carter asked lightly.

"Ridiculously so," I revealed reluctantly.

"Then go after what you really want," he encouraged. "For fuck's sake, you're obnoxiously stubborn when it comes to everything else. And you aren't going to find a better woman. What's the problem?"

"I have no idea how to be Prince Charming," I muttered.

Carter snorted. "I doubt she's looking for the perfect guy."

One guy.

Laura said that was all she wanted.

"I'm not even close to perfect," I said morosely. "Hell, I don't even know how to date anymore. It's been a long time."

"Where are you going for dinner?"

I told him, and watched his face form into an expression of disapproval.

"What?" I asked. "They have great food."

"Maybe. But it's a place where you take businessmen to dinner. It's not very unique," Carter replied.

"What exactly would you suggest?" I asked, my jaw tight.

He was quiet for minute, and he looked like he was thinking before he answered, "How about taking the Bainbridge Ferry? There's some good restaurants on the island."

"I don't take the ferry," I informed him.

"You should," Carter decided. "I think Laura would love it."

"You think so?" He'd gotten me interested in the idea. If Laura really would love it, I'd take the damn ferry.

He nodded. "Definitely. Even though she and Brynn both watch their weight because of their modeling assignments, they're both foodies. And Laura is adventurous."

"Too adventurous at times," I agreed. "She's been all over the world alone." For some reason, it really bothered me to think about Laura being all by herself in a foreign country. Traveling solo wasn't always safe, especially for a female. It left her way too vulnerable.

"Don't think about that too much," Carter advised. "It will make you crazy."

It already did, but I wasn't about to admit that to Carter.

"So let's just say that I took your advice. Where should I make reservations?" I questioned.

He shrugged. "Depends on what kind of food you want."

I brought up my computer and named off several places. Carter helped me choose the best one, and I called for a reservation myself.

"Try to have fun for a change?" Carter suggested as he strode toward the door to get back to his own office.

"I'm not sure I even know how to do that," I mumbled.

"You'll figure it out. I have faith in you," Carter joked.

"Get out of my office," I demanded irritably. "It's still mine until I leave today."

"Don't be pissed off, Mason. Please." Carter's voice was sincere. "And it will always be your office. You'll just be unavailable for a short time. You can thank me for this later."

I wasn't feeling all that gracious at the moment. "Leave."

"Call me tomorrow and let me know how the date goes," he requested.

"I might," I said noncommittally.

Carter didn't say another word as he left and shut the door behind him.

Chapter 11

Laura

"This has been amazing," I told Mason as we sat in a local place on Bainbridge Island for dinner. "How is it that I've been here for two years and never gotten on the ferry before?"

So far, my dinner date with Mason had been full of surprises.

He'd shown up a little bit early with a beautiful bouquet of roses, and he'd looked delicious enough to be on the dinner menu in a dark-gray polo shirt and black jeans.

Since I hadn't known exactly where we were going, I'd opted for a cute sundress. Not too dressy, but good enough if we landed in a nice restaurant.

To say I was surprised when we boarded the ferry was an understatement since Mason had never seemed like an adventurous type of guy.

However, he had seemed to enjoy himself on the ride over.

He shrugged. "I've been in Seattle a lot longer than two years, and I've never been on a ferry, either."

I wasn't terribly surprised about that. I set my utensils on my plate. The fish had been really fresh and delicious, but my belly was full. "What exactly do you do for fun?" I questioned. There had to be something he was passionate about except work.

"Nothing," he answered morosely. "My schedule is set every single day. I get up, work out in my gym at home, go to work and deal with everything that entails, and I go home late and go to sleep. Rinse and repeat the next morning."

"You don't meet up with friends to do anything?"

"I have business acquaintances, not friends. I have a few I keep in contact with from college, but they're on the East Coast."

My heart squeezed, the pressure so tight that I felt like the organ was going to burst. *God, how could anybody live that way?* Yeah, I worked a lot because it was creative, and I loved it. But it wasn't healthy for anybody to work every waking moment of the day. "That's not good for you," I told him firmly. "You need to take some leisure time to recharge."

"And do what, exactly?" he asked.

I was silent as the waitress returned with Mason's credit card and thanked us both for joining them for dinner.

We'd both passed on dessert because the portions and appetizers had been so huge.

"Mason," I said with a sigh. "You're in Seattle. It's an amazing place to live. There's water, mountains, nightlife, incredible museums and exhibits, theater… there's almost nothing you *can't* do here."

"Yeah, well, I'll probably be doing some of it since my brothers decided to boot me out of my office for a week," he said tersely.

I looked at him in surprise. "They what?"

"It seems that they feel the same way you do, and they took the *majority rules* stance today. The bastards," he rumbled. "They're locking me out of my office for a week."

Oh. My. God. "They didn't," I said. "Did they?"

"Yes," he said through his clenched jaw. "But I don't think they realize that I can just work from home. I have everything I need there."

Because I knew Jett and Carter were just forcing a vacation on Mason in the most demanding way possible, I had to bite back a smile. "Don't hate me for saying this," I warned. "But do you really think they haven't covered those bases? Jett is one of the most talented technology guys in the world. I don't know all that much about computers, but it can't be all that difficult for him to change your password or something."

"I'll kill them both if they did," he answered in a cantankerous tone.

"Mason, why are you fighting this so hard? If it helps, I own Lawson stock, and as a stockholder, I totally approve."

He looked taken aback for a second before he responded. "You're invested in Lawson?"

I nodded. "Stock tip from Brynn when we were still modeling full-time. We both bought when you first went public. I've gotten an incredible return on my investment," I answered. "The last thing I want is a burned-out owner at the helm."

"I am not burned out. For fuck's sake, I am only turning thirty-six, not eighty."

I wanted this time off for Mason, so I intended to fight for it. "What if I take some time off with you? We could do some of the fun things in the city together. I mean, I wouldn't take up all your free time, but I could use a break. And unlike you, I realize that my management team can handle things now that I have one in place. Most of my work is more on the creative side."

I had no idea if he even *wanted* a second date, but I was offering more as a friend than a woman who lusted after him. Maybe Mason was still young, but I could see the dark circles under his eyes when I looked beyond his stern expression, and the signs of stress were definitely there on his handsome face.

He looked uptight.

Always.

"You can take up *all* of my free time," he said eagerly. "Jett's gone, and Carter will be at the office every day since Jett and I are both gone."

"Are you willing to go along with anything I want to do?" I questioned, folding my arms across my chest. I wasn't going to let him get away with not going out and exploring to find out exactly what he liked to do. "I'm going to try my best to persuade you to have a life outside the office in the future." *Fair warning.*

"Yes," he said cautiously. "But not the Space Needle and the touristy stuff."

"*Definitely* the Space Needle if you've never been to the top," I insisted.

"I can see the top from Jett's condo, for God's sake. It's a tourist trap."

"But you've never seen the view from the top," I replied persistently. "It's fun."

"Maybe," he said, wavering just a little.

"Tomorrow," I informed him. "Wear something cool. We might have to stand in line for a while."

We were in one of the hottest months, and Seattle was incredibly humid.

"I hate the heat," he argued.

"You'll get used to it," I teased.

"I'm sure I can contact someone—"

"No!" I wagged my finger at him. "You absolutely *are not* allowed to use your influence to get us on and off the top without playing tourist. We're going to be sightseers. *Normal* people."

While it might be tempting to skip the lines, even for me, the crush was all part of the experience. I wanted him to be immersed in what it was like to be...a regular person instead of a billionaire.

"You'll be recognized if we get into that mess," he cautioned. "I'm rarely out there for photos, but your face is everywhere."

"I rarely get bothered in public," I told him. "People are busy with their own lives, and I look different on the street than I do in complete makeup."

"I doubt that. In case I didn't mention it, you look absolutely beautiful tonight."

I felt my face start to heat.

He'd mentioned how great I looked.

At my condo.

On the ferry ride.

On our way to this restaurant.

Granted, I could never say that Mason was smooth, but maybe that's why his compliments made my heart skitter. He really meant them.

"Thank you," I murmured as I glanced at him.

More than my face was getting hot as I watched his eyes caress over me covetously.

I shivered in response. I crossed my legs, uncomfortable as wet heat flooded between my thighs.

All this man had to do was look at me, and I was a mess. He couldn't hide the desire in his tumultuous gaze, and when it landed on my significant cleavage, he didn't look away immediately. It was like he didn't give a damn if he got caught staring at my sizable breasts.

"Um…Mason?" I said breathlessly. "Do we have a deal?"

If he didn't stop looking at me like he owned my body, and coveted every inch of me, I was going to lose it.

"You have your deal." He rose to his feet and held out his hand. "Let's go."

I grasped it like it was my lifeline, and let him lead me out of the restaurant.

We didn't talk much during the walk back to the ferry terminal, but Mason didn't let go of my hand. He simply loosened his grip and let his thumb slide over my skin.

His actions were subtle, but it also felt possessive, and I hated myself for liking that protective hold so much that it made me want to squirm.

I was almost breathless with the desire to throw myself into his arms and beg him to fuck me by the time we got through the boarding process at the terminal, and found a place at the rail for the thirty-minute boat ride back to Seattle.

"We got the best of both worlds," I said with a sigh as the ferry got underway. "It was still daylight when we left, and now we get to see all the lights of Seattle on the way back."

Mason pressed his chest against my back and wrapped his arms around my body from behind. I could feel his warm breath on my neck as he said huskily,. "I won't see the lights. The only thing I can seem to look at is you."

I turned until I was facing him, and his hands grasped the metal rails, trapping me between his arms. "Mason," I groaned, my voice so full of need that I was slightly embarrassed.

His gaze locked with mine, and the chemistry between us was so intense that my entire body tensed up.

Kiss me. For God's sake, kiss me.

The ferry was windy, but at that moment, not a damn thing could make me feel cold.

I was with Mason.

His body was pressed against mine.

And I burned.

Instinctively, I wrapped my arms around his neck because I needed to touch him.

I'd barely had time to stroke the hair at his nape before he said gruffly, "I've been waiting for this all damn night."

His mouth crashed down on mine. There was nothing tentative about his first kiss. He devoured my mouth like he needed to stake his claim.

The kiss was hot, wet, and completely carnal. I parted my lips and let him in, just as hungry for him as he was for me. Maybe more.

I'd wanted this from the moment we'd met, and that desire had sizzled and built every single time I'd talked to him since then. Finally, I could let it all go, and it was a release to just tangle my tongue with his, and at least explore a small part of this big, bold, beautiful man.

There were people wandering around the deck area, but there was nothing except Mason for me at that moment.

I didn't give a damn who saw us.

He commanded my complete attention, and he got it.

I speared my hands into his coarse hair, reveling at the heady sensation of finally getting to know what he tasted like.

His masculine scent surrounded me, and I fell into the embrace like nothing else existed except staying close to him.

He was so big that he made me feel petite, adored, and protected.

I moaned in protest as his lips left mine to explore the sensitive skin of my neck. "Jesus, Laura. It's all I can do to not fuck you right here. Right now," he rasped against my skin, and then grasped my ass to pull me flush with his muscular body.

I closed my eyes as I felt the proof of his desire, his hard cock straining against the material of the denim he was wearing, pressing into the juncture of my thighs. "Mason," I whispered into his ear as I rubbed against him, wanting so much more.

He abruptly stepped back. I was tempted to follow him and keep my body clinging to his, but I didn't.

His breathing was harsh as he raked a hand through his dark hair in frustration. "You're going to fucking kill me someday," he said, his voice grim.

But his eyes…they sizzled with a molten heat that negated the negative comment.

He wanted me just as much as I wanted him, and the naked truth was right there on his face. It was also right beneath those jeans. I'd felt it. I'd rubbed against it. Now I wanted to free him and feel that enormous cock inside me.

I took a shaky breath. "I've never had a public sex fetish," I said, wanting to lighten the mood.

I turned around and gripped the railing, my heart still hammering out of control.

Mason wrapped his arms around my waist, but his hold was lighter this time. "You can make me forget that there's anyone around except you," he whispered huskily into my ear.

My heart skipped a beat. "I don't think either one of us is ready for this to go any further."

Liar. I'm such a liar. I'm almost ready to beg for it.

"Speak for yourself," he grunted. "*I've* been ready for a long time."

He sounded so disappointed that I leaned back against him, and I laughed as we watched the lights of Seattle creeping closer until the ferry ride ended.

Chapter 12

Laura

Laura Hastings Blog Entry, Today, 9 a.m.

Some of you have asked me how I could possibly be insecure, so I'd like to answer that question here today.

I know that I've had a successful modeling career, but believe me, it's fairly easy to feel like the ugly, enormous woman in the room. The modeling world is full of gorgeous women. I'm just a passably pretty face in a crowd of beautiful females who are a whole lot thinner and smaller than I am, which is what is acceptable in the modeling industry. As you all know, I want that to change, but it won't happen overnight.

The thing is, modeling isn't the real world, and I have to remember that. I'm quickly approaching thirty-five, and I've been lucky enough to have a long career for a model. But I'm about ready to retire completely, and I still have a lot of life in front of me.

I guess what I'm saying is that if you are making modeling your career, remember that it's a short-lived endeavor. Use it as a springboard to launch you into a long, successful career doing something else once you retire. But don't take it too seriously, and don't sacrifice any of yourself to be a perfect model because it isn't going to be your career for all that long.

I'm healthy. I'm happy. I love my career, and I love creating fashions that suit women of every shape and size.

But yes, I still have insecurities. I think most women do. The secret is to not let those feelings of being "less than" rule your entire life.

There's so much more to a person than just a body or a face. I think body diversity is something that should be celebrated and not looked down upon in my industry. And I think models need to start looking more realistic and truer to what our world of women actually looks like.

Every one of us is a unique individual, and that's something to be happy about. How boring would the world be if we were all size-two robots who looked exactly the same?

Smile at yourself in the mirror at least once today. You're beautiful, whether you know it or not.

Xoxoxo ~ Laura

"I honestly don't know why you have *any* insecurities," Mason commented as he looked up from his laptop.

After dragging Mason around for four days to play tourist, I was giving him a day of rest at the pool he had at his house—a pool he always had ready, but had never used.

We'd both been swimming, and were now basking in the sun in loungers that were side-by-side.

"Let me guess. You're reading my blog post?" I'd actually been about to doze off, so I hadn't even seen him pick up his computer.

"Of course. I always do."

I couldn't say my relationship with Mason was relaxed, but I loved spending time with him.

He'd complained every single day about attending what he considered tourist attractions, but most of it was teasing. Honestly, I was fairly sure he'd enjoyed the Space Needle, Pike Place Market, and most of the museums and parks I'd hauled him to during the last four days. He'd even let me pull him onto the Seattle Great Wheel because I'd never ridden the gigantic Ferris wheel before.

I made sure we were incredibly busy during the day, and I usually went back to my condo before dinner.

After that incredibly intimate embrace on the Bainbridge Ferry, I'd had a hard time actually relaxing with him. All I could think of was how badly I wanted him to do a whole lot more than just kiss me.

Today was the first day I'd actually allowed myself to wind down by not cramming our day full of activities, and it was proving incredibly difficult since we were lounging half naked by his pool.

Not that he wasn't dressed pretty conservatively in a pair of board shorts, but I had all I could do not to reach out and touch the smooth, damp skin on his muscular, wide chest, or trace every ripped muscle of his abdomen.

He looked impossibly handsome with his hair in disarray, and still wet from his swim.

I sighed quietly, and tried not to remember every time he'd held my hand or given me a scorching hot kiss over the last several days. I failed miserably. He'd kept things light, like he was afraid of scaring me away. But I wasn't the least bit afraid of Mason, except for the fact that he'd be going back to work on Monday, and our stolen time together would be over.

Pulling myself out of my lustful trance, I finally looked away from him and said, "I have had a lot of women ask me how I can have insecurities, and still be a model who appears to be confident in my own skin. I wanted to explain that looking confident and internalizing it are two different things."

"Your post sounded more like a warning to women who want to go into the modeling field," he observed.

"It was," I confirmed. "It really is a short career, and it's not worth destroying your health over. I got caught up in trying to fit into the mold, whether it was good for me or not."

"When do you think you're going to retire completely?" he asked curiously.

"I've been slowly taking less and less work for several years now. My lingerie shoot might be my last gig. I've had a long career. Some models are done by the time they're thirty, or even earlier."

"Are you sad to see that part of your life end?" he asked.

"No. Not really. It would be nice to have a piece of cake and not feel so guilty that I regret eating it," I joked. "I'm really excited about moving on so I can completely focus on my designing. I love to travel, but it would be nice to do it just because I want to go somewhere. I think I'll always be involved in fashion in some way or another, and I'll use every bit of influence and voice I have to try to change the industry, so women aren't killing themselves to be unhealthily thin."

"You've already made some changes to it," Mason observed.

"Not enough," I told him flatly. "Yes, there's a place for bigger models now where there wasn't before, but mostly only for companies who are known for their plus sizes. It's going to take time for an industry to change when it's done things the same way for decades."

"If anybody can do that, you can," Mason said with reassuring certainty.

"Thanks," I said sincerely.

"When do you leave for your lingerie shoot?"

"I have to be in San Diego a week from Monday."

"I'll have my jet ready for you."

It took me a moment to figure out what he was talking about. "Mason, I'm not taking your jet. This is a longtime client, and they cover my expenses. I already have a flight booked."

"Cancel it. It's safer for you to take my jet. My driver can drop you off directly to the aircraft, and I'll have someone pick you up in San Diego. Where are you staying?"

I knew that Mason liked to be in control, but I balked at him planning out *my* schedule. "None of your business," I said coolly. "And I am not changing my plans. I've been running my own life for almost two decades. I've traveled all over the world, and I'm still alive."

"You weren't dating a guy who has made a hell of a lot of enemies during his climb to the top of the heap," he answered in a clipped tone. "We're seeing each other now. You need some kind of security."

I turned my head to look at him, and I realized he was totally serious. The harsh look on his face confirmed it.

"I've never needed security," I argued. "And not a single person has even recognized me while I've been with you. And are we dating? Really? I thought this was just a week-long experiment. Some kind of trial period."

To be honest, I was confused about what Mason and I were to each other. I was the one who had challenged him to spend some time with me and find out if he could enjoy some experiences outside of work.

Obviously, he could.

Regardless of his complaints, he had seemed to enjoy himself this week.

I had no idea if he would have asked me out again if I hadn't thrown out my idea to show him how to see Seattle like a normal person.

He sat up and tossed his towel against the back of his lounger. "It was *always* more than a goddamn experiment to me," he answered, his voice icily cold. "But I guess I should have realized that it was just a game for you since you run away from me like your ass is on fire every single night. I should have understood that you really didn't want to take this any further. I wasn't trying to be controlling, Laura. I was concerned about your safety. I guess I presumed too damn much." He stood up. "I need to take a shower. Since it's getting late, I assume you'll show yourself out."

He didn't wait for me to answer. Mason turned away and walked into the house, but not before I saw a tiny glint of disappointment in his eyes.

His expression had been formidable, but I'd come to know him well enough to recognize that he only resorted to bland indifference when he thought he needed to go on the defensive.

I was still gaping at the sliding door he'd gone through, unable to believe that he'd just…left.

He'd given me no chance to respond or explain.

I continued to gape at the sliding glass door that he'd used to escape inside the house as I thought about what little he'd said.

He's concerned about my safety.

Okay. But he could have found a way better method to explain that to me instead of demanding that I do as he said without any reason why I should.

He's always seen our time together as more than an experiment.

But really, wasn't that exactly what dating really was? A trial to see if two people are good together.

I run away from him like my ass is on fire.

I finally closed my mouth and swallowed hard. Mason had me on that one. I *did* run away from him as soon as our excursions were over.

Our chemistry was just too damn intense.

And that kind of crazy attraction, the type that's deeply carnal and elemental, was so new to me that I didn't know how in the hell to handle it.

I wanted Mason so desperately that I'd had moments when my whole body had started to tremble with longing so intense that it took my breath away.

I'd had to run.

It was either that or tell him how I felt and take a chance.

Problem was, I didn't know if Mason wanted one night, or something more.

Does it matter?

Does anybody know if a relationship is going to last?

I wasn't a damn prude. I was young, I had sexual needs, and until right now, right this moment, I'd tried to assuage them myself since no guy I'd ever dated had ever brought my body to orgasm. Not even close.

I'd had zero O's with a partner.

Mason could do it.

And that was probably exactly what I was afraid of.

If I let myself get too close to Mason, he could break me. That scared the hell out of me.

On the other hand, if I didn't take a chance, I'd never know what could have happened.

Generally, I didn't sleep with a guy after just a few dates. But my situation with Mason was different. It was like we'd had all those Sunday phone calls, and hookups at various family functions as an entire year of foreplay.

He wasn't just some random guy I'd met at a work function.

At some point over the last year, he'd become…important to me. Necessary enough that I'd kept the truth about my decision to have a child from him. Not because it was none of his business what I did. But because I hadn't wanted to lose my connection with him.

So what if it's just one night? At least I'd have that experience. I'd know what it was like to be with a guy who was attracted to me, who apparently gave a damn about me.

And I wanted that. Desperately.

I can't run away this time. I'm not leaving here because I'm afraid that Mason could be the guy who could break my heart.

Dammit. I wasn't the kind of woman who backed down and gave up.

I rose from my lounger and headed for the house. After I locked the slider behind me, I headed for the stairs, knowing I was going to need all of the nerve I could conjure up because I was determined to seduce Mason Lawson.

Chapter 13

Laura

I could hear that the shower was still running before I entered the master bedroom.

I grabbed my bag from the bed that had the clothing I'd taken off when I had changed earlier in the day.

Good. I can get my clothes on for this discussion.

I was fairly comfortable in the modest one-piece swimsuit I was wearing, but I'd feel way better confronting Mason if I could get back into my sundress.

We should talk clothed to avoid distractions, but after that, the clothes are coming back off.

Granted, I'd never actually seduced a man before, but I planned on giving it my best shot.

I was sick of wanting Mason, but not allowing myself to really touch him because I was afraid of rejection. It was beyond time for me to take a chance, and I didn't plan on letting what could be a once-in-a-lifetime opportunity to be with a man who really wanted me just pass me by.

I quickly divested myself of the swimming attire, and snatched up my panties.

What I really needed was a shower. I had to get the chemicals from his pool out of my hair and off my skin.

Later. I can shower later. I have to talk to Mason first.

Just as I decided to forgo looking for another shower in the house, the sound of running water abruptly stopped.

I was so nervous that I simply froze, and hoped he'd stay in the bathroom for a minute.

Unfortunately, he exited about five seconds later with nothing but a towel wrapped around his waist.

Oh. Shit.

I was riveted, and I couldn't have moved a muscle, even if the house was burning down or something.

Mason's short hair was tussled and wet, like he'd already used the towel to run it over his hair. My eyes moved lower, fascinated by the droplets of water clinging to the naked skin of his massive chest.

The towel was slung low on his hips, so I couldn't ignore the small trail of hair that led seductively down to the top of the towel. My body ached with longing to snatch that towel away and see exactly what was hiding beneath it.

I wanted to touch him. *Really* touch him. And it was a struggle to not act on my instincts.

"What in the hell are you doing here? I thought you left," he said harshly.

"I couldn't. Not like that," I said in a husky whisper. God, even my voice was betraying how badly I wanted him. "We need to talk."

Our eyes met. Mine were probably beseeching, but his were still frigidly cold.

"You expect me to be able to have a conversation while you're standing there naked?" he asked hoarsely.

Shit! I'd been so entranced that I'd forgotten I was standing here with my panties in my hand. "I-I'm sorry," I stammered. "I came up to get dressed, and then I thought maybe I needed a shower because of the chlorine, but then I decided to skip it and get dressed so we could talk." I was rattling on, but I couldn't help it.

There was so much tension in the room that it was nearly palpable.

He was staring at me, steadfastly meeting my gaze, but he didn't speak, so I continued. "I wasn't running away, Mason. I swear. The way you make me feel sometimes…scares me. I don't want to make this more than it is because I'm afraid that once this interlude is over, it will hurt not to see you anymore. I don't want to care too much."

I watched, fascinated as every bit of ice in his eyes faded away.

He was suddenly right in front of me, which was shocking for a guy as big as Mason, his gaze intense and warm.

He took me by the shoulders as he said, "Care, Laura. I want you to care because I sure as hell do. This isn't a goddamn game to me. I'm with you every day because I can't imagine having time off and being with anyone else. I. Want. To. Be. With. You. And I have no plans of letting this go after a week. I've wanted you for too damn long to let you go now."

"Then why did you walk away?" I asked quietly.

"Because I'm worried about caring too much, too, if you don't feel the same way I do," he said huskily. "I could tell you were trying to put distance between us. I don't want distance, Laura. I don't need it. I already know what I want."

"What?" I asked, my heart stammering against my chest wall.

His eyes turned stormy and dark as he answered. "You."

"Mason, I—"

I want you to touch me. Really touch me.

"I'm naked," I said weakly.

"Believe me, I noticed," he answered hoarsely.

"I better take a shower." If I didn't get away from him, I'd rip off that towel he was wearing, and fling myself against that gorgeous, enormous body of his. And then I'd beg him to fuck me.

He let go of his grip on my shoulders. "You can use mine," he offered. "If you need somebody to wash your back for you, I'm available."

Moment of truth, Laura. You know what you want, too. Your goal was seduction. Do it!!

I grabbed my clothes from the bed and started toward the bathroom as I said, "I might just need that help."

I caught a glance at his face before I walked through the bathroom door.

"Laura," he said in a warning growl. "I'm not in the mood to joke around."

"I wasn't joking," I said in a firm voice as I partly closed the door behind me.

I went and turned on the shower, and stepped inside, my whole body shaking from the sexual tension that was nearly killing me.

I stood with my back to the water and washed my hair. The more time that passed, the more certain I was that Mason wasn't going to join me, even though he'd been invited.

What if he doesn't know I'm serious?

After all, he *did* seem to think I was kidding.

The tension slowly released as the hot water pounded against my back, and I rinsed my hair.

Maybe it's better this way. Maybe it's too soon. At least I know he isn't just playing with me. That he isn't just killing time with me.

I wasn't about to keep running away from him, though. Not since I'd made the decision that I was willing to take a risk to find out what it would be like to be with a guy like him.

However, we were going to have to discuss his high-handedness. It was nice that he was concerned about me being safe, but he hadn't left any room for discussion.

I squealed loudly as the glass shower door swung open, and a large, naked man entered the big shower. "Mason," I said breathlessly, my heart thundering. "You scared me."

"I hope to hell you were serious when you made that invitation. I stood out there for a good five minutes telling myself that I could wait until you're more comfortable with me, but I don't think I can," he said in a graveled voice.

"I was serious," I said, looking up at the tormented look on his face, an expression that made my heart ache. Mason was a complicated guy, and I knew it wasn't easy for him to express exactly how he was feeling.

But I could see it.

I could feel it.

And his uncertainty made my resolve stronger.

I watched as he pumped liquid soap into his hand and said, "Turn around."

Oh, God. He really was going to wash my back.

I turned around, but not before I got a quick glimpse of his enormously erect cock.

Mason was big *everywhere,* and although his cock was a little daunting, my legs were weak with the need to feel him inside me.

The moment I put my back to him, I shivered at the silky feel of his big hands, slick with soap, running over my skin.

He didn't just touch, he massaged, his hands firm but gentle. Even though all of my senses were heightened, it still relaxed me. "Oh, God, that feels good, Mason," I said, half groaning as his thumb worked a tight muscle in my neck.

He pulled me back against his wet, naked chest and said huskily in my ear, "You're so damn beautiful, Laura. Do you have any idea how many fantasies I've had about this?"

"No," I gasped as he put his hands beneath my breasts and cupped them.

He ran his thumbs over my sensitive nipples as he said, "So damn many times that I stopped counting. In my fantasies, I've fucked you in this shower in every position imaginable, and on every available surface of this house. There isn't a single place that I *haven't* claimed you."

I leaned my head back and closed my eyes. "But this is real."

"Damn right it is," he said in a growl. "And I'm going to make it last just as long as I can."

He turned me in his arms, grabbed my hair, and tilted my head back.

Strangely, when he took control, I melted.

I moaned against his lips as his mouth came down on mine. The kiss was frenzied and frantic, forceful and delicious. I wrapped my arms around his neck and held on for dear life. I opened my mouth and tangled my tongue with his, letting him know without words how desperately I needed to be close to him.

I whimpered as I felt his cock pressed against my belly, and I tried to reach between our bodies so I could wrap my fingers around his hardness.

He lifted his head. "Don't, Laura. Not yet. I have zero control right now."

"I just need to touch you, Mason. I ache..."

"I know. And I need to make you come because I can feel your frustration," he answered as he dropped to his knees.

"Mason, what are you..." My words left me as he buried his face into my pussy, and I realized exactly what he was doing.

Oh. My. God.

His tongue pierced between my folds and invaded the pink, wet, quivering flesh of my pussy, and I moaned with pleasure. "Yes!" My hands grasped his hair and tried to pull his head closer to exactly where I needed it.

But he didn't oblige me right away. His hands slid up the back of my thighs and cupped my ass, as his mouth explored every inch of available pink flesh between my thighs—except for my clit.

I yanked his hair. "Mason. Please."

His touch was sweet torment, and I wasn't sure how much more of it I could take.

I didn't flinch when his fingers dug into my ass and yanked me forward.

I was too ecstatic that his tongue was finally laving over that engorged bundle of nerves that was begging for attention.

Suddenly, that wicked mouth was everywhere, and as my eyes drifted down to watch him feasting on my pussy, I nearly climaxed just from watching the ferocity and concentration in his actions.

Making me come seemed to be his only thought, his only mission, and I was definitely going to give him what he wanted.

"Mason!" I exclaimed in a high-pitched squeal that I didn't recognize as my own.

Watching him on his knees with his dark head between my thighs was too much.

The stimulation of his slick tongue was too much.

His carnal need to watch me come was too much.

I fisted his hair, needing something to ground me.

Mason Lawson was completely primitive at the moment, and I'd never seen or felt anything so pleasurable in my entire life.

The tight-knit ball in my stomach began to unfurl, and the sensations shot straight to my core.

My climax rolled over me with a ferocity that had me mewling and groaning as I helplessly drowned in the pleasure.

Mason eagerly sucked and licked up my juices like they were nectar from the gods, which stretched out the ecstasy for much longer than my climax would usually last.

I was trembling as he rose and wrapped a muscular arm around my waist, which kept me from falling on my ass because my legs had given out.

"Mason," I said with a sigh as I fell against his massive chest.

He turned off the water, and then took my hand while I stepped out of the shower.

Mason quickly dried me off, tossed the towel on the floor, and picked me up and strode from the bathroom.

"Oh, my God. You're going to kill yourself carrying me like this," I warned him breathlessly.

"Then I'll die a very happy man," he answered hoarsely right before he tossed me onto the bed.

Chapter 14

Laura

I was still reeling from the prolonged climax I'd had in the shower, but I wasn't completely satisfied until Mason covered me and I could feel all of that heated, smooth, glorious skin connect with mine.

I wrapped my long legs around his waist to make sure he didn't go anywhere.

I'd been waiting for this.

I'd wanted this for so damn long.

Wrapping my arms tightly around his neck, I insisted, "Fuck me, Mason. Please."

"Christ!" he rasped into my ear. "Do you know how long I've waited to hear you say that?"

"Fuck me," I said again.

"Slow it down, baby," he said huskily. "I'm not a *small guy* anywhere. I don't want to hurt you."

A brief moment of sanity got past my lust-crazed brain, and I realized that Mason was afraid his size was going to be an issue. For me? "You won't hurt me," I groaned. "I'm not small anywhere, either." Granted, I'd gotten a good glimpse of his assets. His cock was enormous, thick, and heavy, but my body was clamoring for him to be inside me. "Please," I pleaded one more time as I lifted my hips.

"Fuck! I can't hold on any longer," he said desperately as he slowly started to enter me.

He's being careful. He's...afraid.

"Don't hold back. Do it," I insisted with a nip to his shoulder.

The tiny love bite seemed to set him off, and he growled as he surged forward and buried himself to the hilt.

"Oh!" I gasped, shocked by the girth and length of Mason.

"Jesus!" he hissed. "You're tight. Did I hurt you?"

I could hear the tension in his voice, and it melted my heart. His entire body was tight. Every muscle bunched up like he was ready to lose it. But didn't. Because he was afraid he'd cause me some pain.

"No," I whispered honestly. Yes, he was big, and my internal muscles were stretching to accommodate him. I'd never been with a man even close to his size, but any discomfort I felt was nothing compared to how good it felt to have Mason inside me. "You feel so good."

He brushed the damp hair from my face, and his beautiful, fathomless eyes met mine. "Laura..." he muttered huskily before he covered my mouth with his.

I fisted his hair, all semblance of patience gone.

I needed him.

He needed me.

And every bit of the sexual tension that had been red-hot between us boiled over as I kissed him back. The embrace was fierce and carnal, like we were both trying to brand each other with our mouths.

I fisted his hair, desperate to alleviate the need that was tearing me apart.

When he released my mouth, we were both panting, and my heart was beating so fast that I felt like it was going to explode from the force of each beat.

"Take what you want, however you want it," I encouraged him.

Truthfully, I wanted to see Mason lose control completely.

I craved it.

"You're going to be damn sorry you said that," he warned as he put a hand beneath my ass to tilt my hips up. "I'll end up fucking you so hard you won't be able to walk for days."

"Worth it," I gasped out as he pulled back until he was almost out, and buried himself again. And then again.

"Yes!" I hissed. "More."

Contrary to whatever Mason thought, he *wasn't* going to break me. I wasn't a fragile Barbie doll.

I looked up at him, his chiseled jawline tight, his eyes murky with the passion that he was allowing himself to unleash. His hair was damp and spikey.

He looked like a madman, and it was so arousing that I moaned.

I kept my legs wrapped around his waist as he started to pound inside me, every thrust driving my crazy desire even higher.

"Mason," I moaned, unable to get anything else out of my mouth.

He was the only thing that mattered at the moment.

He was the only thing I could feel.

He surrounded me.

Overwhelmed me.

Took me places no other man ever had before.

He shifted positions slightly, so the thickness of his cock abraded my clit with every stroke. "Come for me, sweetheart. You're so damn tight, hot and wet that I'm not going to last much longer. Not this time."

His pace was frenzied, and I didn't want him to hold back. But I knew damn well that Mason wasn't going to allow himself to go over the edge until I did.

I moaned at the fast and furious stimulation to my clit, and relished the way our damp skin slid together.

I was close.

So. Damn. Close...

"This changes everything for us, Laura. Now you're fucking mine," he growled, and I could feel those words vibrating through my being.

His caveman, possessive words seemed to send me hurtling into my climax.

"Oh, God. Mason," I screamed as I started to come like I never had before. The pleasure was so intense it was almost painful. My nails dug into the hard muscles of his back, needing something to keep me from flying away from him.

I could feel my internal muscles clamp down on his cock, like they didn't want him to get away.

I tilted my head and watched Mason, his head back, his throat muscles working like he wanted to say something, but couldn't.

"Laura, you're so fucking beautiful," he groaned as my climax milked him of his own hot release.

At that moment, as the crescendo started to wind down to ripples of pleasure, I knew I'd never forget how he'd looked as he said my name, and told me I was the woman he wanted as he was in the throes of his orgasm.

It was the most amazing thing I'd ever experienced.

No man had ever lost himself to…me.

He rolled me on top of him as he moved onto his back, and I ended up sprawled over his massive body, our limbs tangled together as we both tried to recover our breath.

Weary, I tried to move because I wasn't a lightweight.

He slapped me firmly on the ass. "Go anywhere, and I'll come after you," he warned huskily.

"I'll squash you," I said breathlessly. "I'm heavy."

He stroked a hand over my back, a soothing motion that made me relax a little. "You're fucking perfect," he said in a pseudo ornery tone. "Stay where you are. I don't have the energy to chase after you, but I will. I like you exactly where you are."

I actually giggled like a teenage girl as I visualized a cantankerous Mason chasing me around the house naked.

I'd never had a man insist on me being on top of him. Not at my size. But Mason seemed to revel in it.

I sighed as his hand moved lower and stroked over my ass.

"You're probably going to be sore," he said regretfully.

I reached my hand out to stroke his unruly hair. "Why are you so worried about hurting me?"

He hesitated before he finally said, "I usually do hurt women. I'm built like a linebacker, and my dick is proportionate to the size of my body. Too big to feel good for most women."

"Not too big for me," I teased. "Really, Mason, it was incredible. I don't know why on Earth you thought it *wouldn't* be."

He raised a brow like he thought I might be stretching the truth.

"I've had two relationships in my life," he explained. "One right after high school, and one in college. Neither one of them really enjoyed the sex all that much. They said it hurt."

"Let me guess. They were really small women?"

He nodded. "Yeah. I really liked both of them because they were smart, nice women. But in the end, the chemistry just wasn't there."

"So when did you finally find one who appreciated your, um… assets?" I asked curiously.

"Didn't," he muttered.

"What?"

"I said I didn't," he said louder. "Until today."

"All of the women—"

"No more women," he interrupted. "I haven't fucked a woman since I got out of college. Two strikes were enough for me. I stayed busy, too busy for another relationship."

His eyes strayed from mine, and I knew I was hearing something that nobody else knew, something he was, for some reason, embarrassed to admit.

Most men would have had one-night stands or just casual relationships to get laid.

But not Mason.

Just because he'd found two smaller women who hadn't enjoyed a super-sized cock, he'd given up for fear of making another one suffer through it.

I took his face in my hands and urged him to look at me. "Why me, after all those years?"

His eyes met mine as he replied, "Because you're the one woman I couldn't resist. I couldn't get you out of my head."

I felt tears spring to my eyes, but I blinked them back. This was a rare moment of vulnerability for Mason, and I didn't want to screw it up. "I felt the same way. You must have known I was attracted to you."

"I hoped, especially after the night of Jett's engagement party. But then everything changed when you were sober. You were standoffish."

I was taken aback. "What happened at the party?"

"It didn't happen at the party. It happened once I got you home. You seemed to come around after you'd passed out, which meant I didn't need to rush you to the hospital to make sure you were okay. Once I helped you get out of your dress, you were hell-bent on taking me to bed with you. You, Laura Hastings, tried your damnedest to seduce me the night of Jett's engagement party."

Chapter 15

Mason

The night of Jett's engagement party had been heaven, but it had also been pure hell.

I started to explain to Laura what had happened.

I closed my eyes, and I could still play the scene out in my head. I'd been worried about Laura's unconscious state. While I'd been well aware that she was plastered, I'd been pretty damn glad when she'd finally opened those pretty eyes of hers and talked to me.

Until it had come time to take her dress off.

My dick had been so damn hard it would have cut diamonds, and I'd felt like a damn pervert for ogling every beautiful curve she had while she was in a skimpy bra and panties. I mean, what guy wouldn't have looked? However, I wasn't about to take advantage of her drunken state.

"I think you should come to bed with me, handsome," she'd said. "I'm sooo attracted to you. I always have been."

I'd laid her on the bed and covered her with a blanket, but she'd wrapped her arms around my neck. "Kiss me," she'd demanded.

I'd put my hands on her shoulders. "Who am I?" I asked, wondering if she even knew what she was saying.

She'd slapped me on my arm playfully. "I know who you are. You're Mason Lawson. The hottest of the Lawson brothers. Do you know you're the only guy who has ever melted my panties?"

I'd swallowed hard. "No."

"You're ridiculously gorgeous, you're highly intelligent, you're filthy rich, and you're way too unattainable for me, but we could have one night, right?" Her words had been slurred, but her pretty blue eyes had looked at me so earnestly that it had nearly killed me.

"Not tonight," I'd said huskily as I kissed her forehead. "If you feel the same way when you're sober, tell me, and then we'll talk."

I'd pulled back, which had taken a Herculean effort, and waited until she'd finally fallen to sleep.

I felt Laura roll off me after I'd finished explaining, but she didn't go far. She curled up next to me and buried her face in my chest as she moaned, "Oh, my God! I didn't!"

"You did," I answered mischievously. "You have no idea how hard it was not to crawl into that bed with you that night. But you were drunk. And once you were sober, you were distant, and you never mentioned that attraction again. Not that I didn't give you plenty of chances. I did call you every Sunday."

"Only to see if I was pregnant," she complained.

"Actually, I think I was waiting to see if you brought up that night. But you didn't. I figured you weren't really interested."

She lifted her head and looked at me. My damn heart almost jumped out of my chest. "You're kidding, right?" she asked. "And *you* could have said something."

I shrugged. "I thought you were embarrassed about it, and didn't want to discuss it. Until you recently told me you didn't remember anything about that night after we talked on the patio."

"You could have told me then," she said firmly.

"What did it matter? Why embarrass you when I thought you weren't interested?"

"I was always attracted to you, Mason. But you were all business until you decided to lobby to be my baby daddy."

I grimaced. "Bad move."

"Do you want to tell me why you really did that?" she asked hesitantly. "I was shocked that you were willing to give me so much personal information."

No, I really *didn't* want to tell her because I was having the most amazing night of my life, and I didn't want to spoil it. However, I wasn't going to lie—or even stretch the truth—with Laura again. "Honestly, I couldn't stand the thought of you getting pregnant unless the guy who knocked you up was me. That's how damn crazy you make me sometimes."

"Oh," she said simply, sounding surprised.

I rolled onto my side and propped my head up with my hand. "I know I handled things badly earlier tonight, but it's like I can't control myself when it comes to you being safe. Maybe some of that fear comes from the fact that I lost my parents in the blink of an eye. I know how fragile life can be. I feel protective and possessive with you, and I think that now that I've claimed you as mine, it's going to get even worse. I'm not even going to pretend that it's going to be easy being in a relationship with me, but it has to be all or nothing for us, Laura. Which way will it be?"

Dammit! The last thing I wanted was to scare her away, but I knew I had to warn her that those instincts would never be far from the surface for me. Not with her. Not ever.

Her eyes widened. "Are we…in a relationship?"

"I sure as hell hope so," I growled. "And I won't share with other men. I can't."

Oddly, she didn't look the slightest bit frightened. In fact, she smiled, and my damn heartbeat kicked into overdrive as her lips kept turning up.

She wrapped a hand around my neck and fingered the hair at my nape as she said, "Good thing," in a voice that seduced me. "Because I'm not sharing, either. It's going to be all for me, Mason. With you, it has to be. Monogamous, until one of us feels differently. Deal?"

I lowered my forehead to hers in relief. "Deal. If I start being an asshole, just tell me."

"Oh, you know I will," she said with a laugh. "Next time, please explain before you give orders. We can *discuss* it. I'm not going to promise I'll do what you say, but at least I might get where you're coming from. I lost my parents the same way, and I get how terrifying it can be to think about losing someone else you care about.

I pulled my head back to look into her eyes. I nearly drowned in the depths of her gorgeous blue eyes. "You're a beautiful woman, Laura, and I hate the thought of you being alone and vulnerable. And now, it's going to be known that you're important to me. I don't want anything to happen to you. Even Carter sends security with Brynn when she's traveling, and he can't be with her for the whole trip. And Jett keeps a tail on Ruby, too."

I could see her brain working behind those intelligent eyes of hers. And I just hoped to hell she'd see reason. If not, we were going to end up fighting before the relationship part really began.

I fucking knew that I wanted to give Laura any damn thing she wanted, but the fact was, I was a rich, powerful guy, and I had made enemies. Probably a whole lot more than Jett and Carter since I dealt more with the ruthless business part of our company.

Jett was the tech genius.

Carter was the marketing genius.

And me? I was the business muscle.

I had more enemies than Jett and Carter combined.

"Okay, I'll use your jet," she said in a contemplative voice. "And I'll take your car to and from my accommodations. But no security tail. Mason, I know San Diego well. I've done a ton of shoots there over the years, and I do have a couple of business meetings. I need to conduct myself like a businesswoman, and that doesn't mean having my guy's security on my ass."

Preferably, I'd way rather be all over Laura's luscious ass myself, but I had some meetings during her trip that I couldn't miss myself.

I looked at her face, and she seemed like she had moved as much as she was going to compromise. "Deal. But check in with me so I know you're doing okay," I grumbled.

"Every day," she promised. "I'd want to know if you were doing okay, too, if you were out of the state or the country. It's reasonable. But I have one more request."

Hell, I didn't feel the least bit *reasonable*. But I was glad she *thought* I was. "What's that?" *Like there was anything I wouldn't do for her.* Whatever she wanted; she could consider it done.

"Don't treat me like I'm fragile, Mason. I'm stronger than you think. And I want you just as much as you want me. I've never done it, but I think I'd like any kind of down and dirty sex that you want to try." She paused before she continued. "It feels really good to know you want me that much."

All I want is a man who's attracted to…me.

She'd said something like that when I'd asked her what she wanted in a man. What in the hell had been wrong with the men she'd previously dated? With her beautiful blonde hair, and soulful blue eyes, she looked like a damn angel with killer curves.

She was soft where I was hard, and she felt like a wet dream with her velvety skin pressed against me when we were skin-to-skin, and those curves would mold perfectly against me even when we were clothed. And then, I'd *wish* I had her naked.

"You have to know you're beautiful, Laura. You've had a very long career as a supermodel. That wouldn't have happened if you weren't a damn head turner, no matter what size you wear. I guarantee there are more men than just me who want to get you naked. A lot more." Unfortunately, just the thought of those men made me want to lose it.

"The only one I care about is you," she murmured as she put her hand to my whiskered jawline.

"This…you…it's one of the best things that's ever happened to me," I told her honestly. "I don't want to screw it up. But I'll try to remember that you actually prefer a guy with a big dick."

She snorted. "Don't you forget it, mister," she teased. "So what are we doing tomorrow?"

I grinned at her. "Sunday. We have a standing date at six o'clock, but I'd rather you stay here until tomorrow."

I wanted the next twenty-four hours solid with this woman more than I wanted to fucking breathe.

She nodded. "I want to stay. Other than earlier tonight, I've had an amazing time this week with you. Are you missing the office?"

Weirdly enough, I couldn't say that I really *had* missed being at Lawson. Maybe it had felt strange at first, but I trusted Carter. And I was pretty sure my absence hadn't collapsed the company.

"Not really. I had a very attractive distraction," I answered honestly. "And I'm not going to work every moment of the day anymore, Laura. I want to have some time and energy left for you. I'll probably still work harder than my other two slacker partners," I joked. "But they're right—we all need some time to breathe."

"So where are we breathing tomorrow?" she asked with a seductive smile that got my dick harder than a rock.

I fell to my back and pulled her luscious body on top of mine. I wanted her to ride me until we were both spent and exhausted.

"Do you really think we'll ever make it out of this house?" I said in a husky, horny voice.

Hell, no matter what she said, I was going to have to keep my dick in my pants occasionally over the next twenty-four hours. She was so damn tight, and I knew she hadn't been with anybody since... *James? Jason? Justin?* Whatever his name was—the stupid fucker who hadn't known how good he'd had it.

Maybe I had promised to give her everything I had, but we could work up to that slowly.

She slid off me. "I think we need another shower now. It's my turn to...wash your back."

I swallowed hard as I saw her sensual smile.

Holy hell. She didn't think she was going to actually...

I had to hold back a groan when images of Laura—naked, wet, on her knees with my cock in her mouth—assaulted my brain. "No," I told her firmly as I stood up, and then pulled her up from the bed. "You'll gag. It wouldn't be pleasant."

"On the contrary," she said in a silky voice. "I think you'll find it *very* pleasant."

I'd probably start to come the minute I felt her wet, hot mouth on my cock since I was a blowjob virgin. No woman had ever cared enough to even try to take me on.

"That's not the point," I said, trying to keep my voice stern.

She took my hand. "It's *exactly* the point. I want to pleasure you, too, Mason."

Fuck! How could I explain to her that she gave me pleasure just by being close to me and breathing?

She tugged on my hand, and I followed her because I simply couldn't *not* follow Laura.

"Don't worry," she cooed as she turned on the water. "I'm an intelligent woman. I think I can figure out how to make it feel good."

She did.

In fact, she entirely blew my mind.

Chapter 16

Laura

"Oh, my God," Brynn said as we met over coffee the following Tuesday afternoon. "You actually tried to seduce Mason when he took you home from Jett's engagement party?"

I smiled. "Yes. Apparently, I did. I don't remember it, but I'm sure Mason isn't making it up."

Although I wasn't about to share all of my intimate moments with Mason, just like Brynn didn't share all of hers with Carter, there were things I'd tell her that I wouldn't share with anyone else.

Like that mortifying moment when Mason had told me that I'd tried to pull him into my bed while I was in a drunken stupor.

And I'd definitely never even whisper about how I'd felt when Mason had finally let go and orgasmed with my lips wrapped around his massive cock. He'd been wet, hot, and out of control, every muscle in his body tense as he'd groaned out my name in a guttural voice that had shaken me to my core.

Only later had he admitted that it was a first for him, which I'd found as heartbreaking as it was arousing.

Brynn snorted. "Oh, Laura. That's priceless. Well, at least you know what happened that night now."

"And it *was* Mason, so I know he didn't take advantage of the situation," I said with a smirk as I took a sip of my coffee. "He might be high-handed, but the man has a conscience."

"So how was your week together?" Brynn asked curiously.

My best friend had been gone for the better part of last week on a shoot, so we were trying to catch up on everything.

I sighed. "It was fantastic. I dragged him around to a ton of tourist stuff, and although he griped about it, he had a good time."

"I think you had fun, too," Brynn observed.

"I did."

"Let me guess," Brynn said. "You're crazy about him."

"Is it that obvious?" I asked.

"To me, yes. I've known you for a long time, Laura. You're glowing. And it has nothing to do with your makeup."

"He's so different once you get past that arrogant shell of his. We've decided to give this relationship a shot. Monogamous. No dating other people. Like I *could* date another man? Mason is *the* fantasy, bossy or not."

Brynn shot me a genuine smile. "For once, I'll approve of your boyfriend."

"Sometimes it's just hard to believe that he really wants to be with just me," I confessed. "I mean, he's Mason-Fucking-Lawson. There probably isn't a single woman in the entire world who wouldn't do almost anything to be with him. He's hot, he's brilliant, he's young, and he's a billionaire at the helm of one of the biggest tech companies in the world."

"You're hot, you're brilliant and talented. You're young, and you're wealthy. You're the perfect couple. But I don't think you care about all that stuff, do you?" Brynn questioned.

I shook my head. "I don't. I like him because he makes me feel beautiful, sexy, and special. I couldn't care less about his money or his power. I care about the man he is."

"I think once a Lawson man finds the woman who makes him crazy, they're done. Carter makes me feel that way, too. There could be hundreds of beautiful women in the room, but he'll pass them all by until he finds…me. It's like no other woman exists except me."

"Exactly," I said, nodding my head. "Sometimes, it's a little scary."

Brynn laughed. "You'll get used to it, and then you'll love it."

"I think I already love it," I confessed. "I mean, what woman doesn't want to feel like she's the only woman her man sees?"

"None," Brynn agreed. "Except it's not easy to find a guy like that. Wait until he starts doing a bunch of sweet things just so that you know he's thinking about you, even when you aren't together."

"He already did. He sent flowers to me yesterday while I was working at home, and all the card said was *Hello, Beautiful*. Two words, and a couple of dozen roses, and I was sappy for the entire day. But doesn't it ever get scary? I mean, if a man becomes your entire world like that, the fall could be pretty hard if it doesn't work out."

Brynn laughed. "Oh, it will work out. The Lawson men aren't quitters. If you get in a fight, they'll find a way to fix it. They're tenacious that way."

"They're all intense," I observed.

"That, too," Brynn replied. "But Mason will never leave room for doubts about whether or not he gives a damn, and I doubt he'll ever want you to change."

I thought about every other male in my life as I told her, "He doesn't. I don't think he ever would. He accepts me exactly the way I am. He's good at making me feel like the sexiest woman on Earth."

"Perfect," Brynn said as she beamed at me. "Exactly the type of guy you need."

I hesitated before I asked, "Doesn't it ever make you crazy that Carter wants you to have security on your tail?"

"No. Not anymore," she said thoughtfully. "At first, I hated giving up my freedom to wander wherever I wanted to go. We fought about it. It took me awhile to realize it was just going to be one of those compromises I had to make. I wouldn't want to be terrified all the time that something would happen to Carter because of me, so I get why he wants to make sure I'm okay. Really, it's a small trade-off for his piece of mind. He doesn't get too crazy with the security. It's only hard for him when I'm traveling. I've learned to pretty much ignore my tails when I'm traveling on assignment."

I let out a long breath. "I'm only taking Mason's jet and his transportation in San Diego. I know the city so well."

"And Mason was okay with that?"

I smiled. "He didn't have much choice. It was our compromise. Besides, this is my last gig. I've decided I'm ready to take myself out of that world completely now."

"Really?"

I nodded. "I've had a long career, and I'm ready to let it go so I can move on. I'd like to have a piece of cake occasionally without freaking out about fitting into the fashions I have to model. I've spent the last seventeen years or so trying to be the woman the fashion industry wanted. I think I'm ready to just be who I am now."

"That's fantastic, and funny, too. I just did my last assignment for almost the same reasons," she confided. "I love designing my bags, and the demand keeps growing. I want to focus completely on my business."

I grinned at her. "Me, too."

"So what are you going to do about all the fertility clinic stuff now that you're seeing Mason?" Brynn asked.

"I have to tell you something," I said, my tone more serious. "I gave up on the idea of artificial insemination awhile ago. I just didn't feel like it was the right thing to do for me."

I continued to explain to Brynn everything I'd told Mason until I'd gotten all of my feelings on the subject out.

"Why didn't you tell me?" she asked quietly once I'd finished explaining. "I would have understood. I think it's amazing that you want to adopt from the foster care system."

"I guess I felt a little silly and selfish. Not to mention the fact that I still hadn't told Mason, and he was calling me about it every week."

She shot me a knowing glance. "You didn't want him to stop calling you," she guessed.

"As pathetic as it might sound, I didn't," I acknowledged ruefully. "I did have a thing for him, Brynn. I just didn't want to admit it. Not to myself or anybody else."

"But you know it now. And when you and Mason get married—"

I held up my hand. "Whoa, girl. We're just barely exclusively dating. No discussions about marriage have happened. At all."

Brynn frowned. "I'm just saying that you could end up having a child of your own, too."

"Let's just see what happens, okay? Hell, I'm not even used to Mason and me being a couple. I really am okay with adopting. I honestly want to do it. But now that I'm not worried about my biological clock ticking louder every day, I can wait."

I'd already told Mason that I still had an effective IUD, so pregnancy wouldn't be an issue. We'd gotten so caught up in each other last Saturday night and Sunday, he'd never even asked until we'd parted ways on Sunday night.

"Whatever you decide, you'll be an amazing mother, Laura," Brynn said softly. "I don't think your reasoning was all that selfish. But as your friend, I've always wanted to see you get the whole package. A man who loves you, *and* children you can raise together, whether they're biological or not."

I felt like my heart was being squeezed inside my chest. Brynn would probably never know how much her friendship and support meant to me. "Thank you," I said sincerely.

"I never would have made it through my modeling career without you," Brynn said in a tearful voice. "It really feels right that we're completely retiring together. I think we're both ready to turn the page and start a new chapter in our lives, without the restrictions of modeling hanging over our heads."

"I think so, too," I told her, feeling a little teary myself.

Brynn and I had been through everything together, and most likely, we'd saved each other's lives when we made our pact to turn things around and start worrying about our health.

"So, how about a piece of pie with this coffee?" Brynn said mischievously.

My immediate reaction was ingrained, and I almost said no out of habit.

I hadn't been starving myself, but I'd been on a strict diet with very few exceptions for years.

It was time to start saying yes once in a while.

"I'm doing the caramel apple pie," I said with a grin. I'd seen a customer with a piece when I'd entered the restaurant, and I'd nearly salivated over it before I saw Brynn at our table.

"Where's the damn menu?" Brynn said right before she snatched it from the end of the table and started browsing the desserts enthusiastically.

Oh yeah, it was definitely time for Brynn and me to loosen up about counting every single calorie, and start living our lives.

Chapter 17

Laura

At exactly six p.m. the following Sunday, I smiled as I rifled through my purse to grab my ringing cell phone.

I didn't stop walking. It was a beautiful day in Seattle to be outside. But I did slow down my pace so I could chat.

"You know, you really can stop calling me every Sunday at the same time now that we see each other every single day," I said with a laugh after I answered the phone.

"Maybe I just called to talk dirty to you," he answered mischievously.

I rolled my eyes. Like he didn't already do *that* every single day? But I guess I was always open to more of it.

"Before you start that, we need to talk about you sending me every single thing I talk about or look at when we're together," I admonished. "I'm going to run out of room to put all of your gifts in my condo."

Every day, it was something different. Today, I'd had three deliveries.

I'd mentioned to Mason that I needed to go look at new refrigerators. A very top-of-the-line fridge had been delivered this morning.

I'd also made the mistake of taking a long glance at a beautiful pair of silver earrings in a store window while I was with Mason. Those had arrived at noon.

Because I obviously hadn't learned my lesson yet, I'd complained about a silly little glitch with my computer. The new one had come to my door at four p.m.

It had been much of the same almost every day this week.

Honestly, it had to stop. Not that it didn't almost bring tears to my eyes that Mason listened carefully to every damn thing I said, and wanted to make my life easier, but he already pleased me in so many ways. I didn't need those gifts.

"It's not like it's difficult to order that stuff," Mason grumbled. "I want you to have what you need."

I snorted. "I have everything I *need*. The earrings were a *want* that I didn't have to indulge. If I bought every pair of earrings I look at, I'd be filling up a huge jewelry box."

"I'll send you a big one tomorrow," he answered.

"No! Oh, my God, no," I told him firmly, but I was smiling even broader. He got to me hard because he was so willing to do anything to make me happy. "Mason, all I need is you. I have plenty of money. I can buy everything I want or need except...you."

God, I was so crazy about this man who was so willing to give me anything I wanted before I even knew that I wanted it. Mason had a huge heart that very few people ever got to see, and I adored him for it. However, he needed to understand that I didn't *want* all that stuff. Just having *him* was more than enough.

"I like taking care of you," he mumbled.

"And I like that you want to do that, but it's not necessary. Really. But thank you. The earrings are gorgeous."

"Are you wearing them?"

"Yes." I stopped abruptly after I ran up a few stairs. "Do you want to see them?"

"Damn right I do," he growled as he opened the front door of his home and appeared right in front of me.

I disconnected the call, and dropped my cell into my bag. "Happy birthday," I said with an enormous grin that I couldn't seem to wipe off my face when he was around.

I had to wonder if there was ever going to be a day when my heart didn't do a happy dance every time I saw his handsome face.

Probably…not.

He was dressed casually in a pair of jeans and a gray T-shirt that seemed to lovingly hug the enormous muscles in his biceps and chest.

But the thing that *really* got my heart racing was the big, happy grin on his face as he put his cell phone into the pocket of his jeans before he reached out and grabbed all the bags in my arms.

I was making him dinner, and I'd picked up a cake from a bakery right down the street.

I'd used Uber today since I knew that Mason wanted to take me to the airport in the morning.

"Did you walk?" he asked as he put the bags he'd taken from me on the kitchen counter.

"Only from the bakery. It's right down the street. Now that I'm doing my last modeling gig, and I plan on enjoying life with a little chocolate, I need to up my exercise whenever I can. And it's gorgeous outside."

"I missed you," he said in a low baritone voice that always made my toes curl.

He slipped his arms around me, and I wrapped mine around his neck as he gave me a soul-stealing kiss that took my breath away.

When he finally lifted his head, I reminded him, "I just saw you last night."

I'd had to wrap up some work at home today because I was leaving for San Diego in the morning, so I'd returned to my condo last night.

He kissed my forehead. "I can help you out with the whole exercise thing."

The muscles in my thighs still burning from the night before, I laughed. "You already have. And it's your birthday, so I'm cooking you dinner. Don't start getting me distracted." I teasingly pushed him away so I could start unpacking the stuff to make him lasagna, one of his favorites.

Mason was an insatiable lover, but I sure as hell wasn't complaining. The man made me feel like a goddess because he couldn't stop touching me, and I doubted I could ever get enough of him.

Just a kiss, and his seductive, masculine scent was enough to make me want to do him right here in the kitchen.

I knew I couldn't keep touching him, or his birthday dinner wouldn't happen until midnight.

He leaned against a counter and watched me. "I wish you would have called me. I could have walked you back here."

"Mason, it's a short walk. And it's daylight. I wasn't going to have you come pick me up for a five-minute walk."

"I would have come," he protested.

I turned to him and put a palm to his scruffy jawline. "I know you would have," I said with a sigh. "But I've been an independent woman my entire life. The thought of calling you to walk with me for five minutes wouldn't even occur to me. You have to understand that I'm used to being alone."

I kind of had a love/hate relationship with his protective nature. I loved that he cared enough about me that he didn't want anything to happen to me. But I hated the fact that he thought I should be protected every minute of the day.

He caught my hand and kissed my palm. "And I need *you* to understand that you're not alone anymore, and I can't stand the thought of anything happening to you," he answered, his eyes appearing to darken at the idea that somebody might harm a single hair on my head.

Mason was intense when it came to keeping me safe and happy, and I didn't want to change the way that he cared about me. I loved it. But I wanted to keep reminding him that I was almost thirty-five years old, and I'd managed to take care of myself for this long without much mishap.

"Nothing is going to happen to me," I reassured him as I stroked my hand over his whiskered jaw.

"It better not, or I'd be fucking useless," he answered hoarsely. "I need you, Laura."

I took my hand away, and tenderly kissed his lips before I told him, "I need you, too, Mason."

That vow was nothing but the truth. In a very short period of time, I'd come to rely on Mason's affection, and I didn't want to imagine my life without it.

He was the best part of every day for me.

For a woman who had never really had that kind of devotion, that kind of affection, he was like a balm to my soul.

Not to mention a huge help for my insecurities.

Slowly, Mason was breaking down those negative body images I'd always had. No matter how much I'd tried to rid myself of them entirely, they'd always been there. Now, he'd made me love my body because it fit so well with his, and the pleasure we'd found with each other was nothing less than incredible.

Mason made me feel beautiful and sexy. To him, I *was* irresistible. And since I was crazy about him, his opinion was the only one that really mattered.

"Laura," he said in a guttural voice as he looked at me like he wanted to say something.

Instead, he snaked a hand behind my head and kissed me.

I was lost the moment that strong, demanding mouth covered mine.

I clung to him as he ravaged my senses, letting myself become engulfed in the red-hot chemistry that always flowed between the two of us. I speared a hand through his hair, needing to get as close to him as I possibly could.

But it just wasn't enough.

I wanted to climb inside him and never come out.

We were both panting when he raised his head and started to devour every inch of bare skin he could find. Since I was wearing a sundress with spaghetti straps, it wasn't all that hard to find a lot of places to put that hot, scorching mouth of his.

I let out a long, needy moan as his hands went to my ass, and he pulled me flush against his groin and ground his hips against mine.

"That's what you do to me, sweetheart," he growled. "All I can think about is getting inside you."

"Mason," I panted as I yanked on his hair. "Please."

"Please, what?" he demanded to know.

"Fuck me," I insisted.

He lifted me up and sat me on the kitchen counter. The second his hands were free, they were tearing at my sundress, and jerking it over my head.

I released a satisfied sigh as his hands cupped my breasts and his mouth covered one of my hard nipples. I put both of my hands in his hair in encouragement.

He licked, sucked, and nipped, moving from one breast to the other, until I was nearly mad with lust.

"What in the fuck am I going to do without you for a week," he grumbled as his hand slid down my body and into my panties.

Waves of pleasure coursed through my body as he slipped his fingers into my slick pussy.

"Think about *this*?" I suggested. "Fuck me, Mason."

"Damn right I'll be thinking about this," he said hoarsely as he straightened up and yanked my panties down my ass and legs until they dropped to the floor.

He fumbled briefly with the buttons of his jeans as he added, "Every single night. All I think about is you. This. *Us*."

I gasped when he drove himself home, even though I was ready for it.

"Did I hurt you?" he asked, his body suddenly tense.

I wrapped my legs around his waist. "No. Don't you dare go anywhere," I said in a threatening voice.

When a man like Mason buried himself to his balls inside me, there was no way I wasn't going to react. Not because it hurt, but because it hurt so damn good.

It always took an instant for my body to accommodate his because of his size, but after that, it was pure bliss.

I ground against him, and he finally snapped and started to thrust inside me.

Over and over.

Driving me higher and higher.

He kissed me, his tongue working at the same tempo as his cock, and I could feel my climax approaching so quickly that it was almost frightening.

"You feel so damn good, baby," he said huskily as his lips left mine.

I tilted my head back until it hit the cupboard, and when Mason devoured the sensitive skin of my neck, I reveled in it.

There was something incredibly hot about being completely naked while Mason was fully clothed. His hands stroked over the naked skin of my back, but all I could feel was rough denim and cotton. I wanted to touch him, but I couldn't get to his skin, so I was completely focused on where our bodies met intimately.

I was half crazed by the time my orgasm started to wash over me.

"Yes. Oh, God, yes," I screamed. "Mason..."

I came around his cock, and a moment later, he found his own release. "Laura," he said in a throaty, tortured groan.

In that moment, there was only the two of us, caught up in a passion so intense that I felt mindless.

My head dropped to his shoulder as he stayed lodged inside me, his arms tightly around my body.

"One of these days, you're going to kill me," he rumbled against my neck.

I smiled against his skin because he didn't sound the least bit afraid of dying from too many orgasms.

Once I caught my breath, I murmured, "I think dinner is going to be a little late."

"Don't care," he answered as he lifted me, and I slid down his body until I found my feet. "You're the best damn birthday gift. Ever."

I grinned at him as he gently picked up my panties and helped me step into them, and then grabbed my sundress and pulled it over my head.

Considering Mason's appetite, and the fact that I was making his favorite dish, it was probably one of the best compliments I'd ever gotten.

Chapter 18

Laura

"So what do you want to know about Perfect Harmony, Mr. Montgomery?" I queried politely as I sipped a glass of white wine.

We'd scheduled our lunch meeting in San Diego at a nice Italian restaurant close to downtown.

Hudson Montgomery was charming as hell, and better-looking in person than in his pictures. But our choice of Italian food just reminded me of Mason, and how much I missed him.

Especially when Hudson had ordered the lasagna.

God, I'm completely pathetic.

I reminded myself that it was only two more days until I'd see Mason again, and tried to focus on the guy across from me who had asked for this appointment.

Hudson Montgomery was breathtakingly attractive, but he did absolutely nothing for me. Logically, I could understand how some women might swoon over him. His dark locks were cut short, and he appeared to be impeccably groomed in a dark suit and tie. His facial bone structure was perfection, and he probably would have had an amazing career in modeling if he wasn't a billionaire businessman. He was tall and muscular, but not as imposing as Mason.

Aesthetically, he was nearly flawless, and nice eye candy, I supposed. But there was only one man who got a reaction from me, and he was over twelve hundred miles away.

I waited and watched as Hudson tossed back half of his tumbler of whiskey before he spoke. "I have a confession to make, Ms. Hastings," he said smoothly.

"Please, call me Laura," I requested.

He nodded sharply. "And I'd like it if you'd call me Hudson."

"So what's your confession, Hudson?" I asked curiously.

His eyes stayed focused on my face as he answered, "I didn't ask you here to talk about your company, even though I'm incredibly impressed by what you've done with it so far."

"Why am I not completely surprised about that?" I said drily. "I thought it was a little strange that a businessman of your caliber was inquiring about my business. I am still a fledgling company."

Then what in the hell does he want?

As I surveyed the tall, dark, and gorgeous man across from me, I couldn't quite figure out why he unnerved me just a little. He'd been perfectly polite since the moment we'd sat down and ordered lunch and our drinks. But when our gazes met and held for a moment, I suddenly noticed that his eyes were gray, just like Mason's.

It's his eyes.

They were *familiar*, the shape and color so similar to Mason's.

"Actually," he started to explain, "I'm aware that Mason Lawson invested a significant amount of money into your company, so I'm curious as to how well you know each other."

I hated the fact that I just couldn't read Hudson's face, nor could I interpret what he was thinking by looking into his eyes like I could with Mason. I had no clue where all of this was going. His face was stony, and it was impossible to find any kind of emotion in his expression.

"I can't think of why that would be any of your business, Mr. Montgomery." Okay, yes, I was defensive when anybody tried to get information about Mason. Especially billionaire businessmen who could very well have a nefarious motive.

"How well do you know each other?" he pressed.

I frowned. "Well enough that I'm not about to give you any information that isn't common knowledge," I said snippily as I started to stand up. "I think this meeting is over."

It was obvious to me that he was using me to get info on Mason, and *that* definitely wasn't going to happen.

"Wait," he said urgently. "Don't go. I'm not trying to get business dirt on Mason. I promise. I don't operate that way."

I hesitated. "You either stop playing games and tell me what you want, or I'm leaving."

"Please sit," he said politely.

"Talk first," I demanded.

He grinned. "No wonder Mason was looking at you like he was crazy about you in those wedding pictures of Jett Lawson's that I saw in the gossip columns. Stand down, Laura. I'm not competition to Lawson Technologies. Mason Lawson is my cousin."

I was so surprised that I did sit back down. "What? How?"

"I didn't intend to spill that information, but I didn't want you to walk out the door before I could ask you a favor. Whatever your relationship is with Mason, I'm hoping you can try to convince him to return my calls. I've been trying to connect with him for over a year. We spoke once, but he told me that he had his own family, and he wasn't interested in getting to know me or my brothers. But I'd really like to get to know him and his siblings."

"So you're related to him through his biological father," I muttered, trying to figure out exactly what was going on.

"You know that he's adopted?" Hudson said with surprise in his voice. "He said none of his siblings knew."

I nodded. "That's true. They don't. He doesn't want to tell them."

"So would I be wrong to assume that you and Mason are close?"

"We are," I admitted.

"So can you give me any clue why Mason doesn't want to be part of our family? Hell, we don't have to act like we grew up together or anything, but it would be nice to be…friends. I just found out that he existed last year when I finally cleaned out some of my deceased father's journals that had been stored away for years. He mentioned Mason, or I still wouldn't have known I had a cousin out there that I'd never met. I called him soon after I found out, but he was really standoffish, which I thought was strange. It's not like me or my siblings have done anything to cause him to be so aloof that he didn't want to get to know us."

I felt bad because Hudson sounded slightly injured. "I don't know much, either," I confessed. "He said his real father was an asshole. So I'm guessing that he just wants to stay away from the entire family."

"He doesn't want to know anything about the other side of his biological family?" Hudson questioned.

I shrugged. "Apparently not, and I think that's *his* decision to make."

Although I felt that it might be nice if Mason would give a relationship with his cousins a shot, knowing Mason, he probably felt it would be a betrayal to his brothers and sisters if he did.

Yeah, the logic was a bit twisted, but Mason was fiercely loyal to his family.

Hudson reached into his pocket and handed me his card. "It has my personal number on the back," he said. "If Mason ever changes his mind, he can get ahold of me. I haven't shared the information with my brothers or my sister, Riley. There's no point if Mason isn't willing to get together. It would just hurt their feelings if he wanted nothing to do with them."

I took a deep breath, and chose my words carefully. "It isn't personal, Hudson. And it has nothing to do with your family. But he doesn't have a good impression of his bio dad." Really, that was as much as I could reveal.

Hudson nodded. "With good reason. My uncle *was* an asshole, from what I understand. He died the year I was born. My father was pretty much cut from the same mold. But I'd like to think my generation all turned out okay."

"Mason is a very good man," I felt compelled to tell him. "And his siblings are amazing, too. Like I said, it's nothing personal. He's not blowing you off because he's trying to be a jerk. I just don't think he's completely okay with being adopted. He didn't find out until he was almost finished with college."

"Ouch," Hudson said sympathetically. "So he's still trying to deal with that?"

"I think so," I said noncommittally as I put his card in my purse. "Be patient. He might come around some day. I'm hoping he'll tell his siblings eventually. It won't matter to any of them. He's always going to be their brother. It's a difficult situation because he loved his adoptive father very much. He was the man who raised him, and loved him until the day he died in an accident, along with Mason's mother."

"I get it," Hudson answered. "He's had a lot of shit to deal with over the last decade or so. I guess I understand why he's never returned my calls after our initial discussion. But I don't have to like it."

I wondered if Hudson knew the whole story about how Mason's mother had gotten pregnant, but I didn't want to pry into the details. That was something Mason and Hudson would need to talk about if Mason decided he wanted to know more about his bio family.

"I'm sorry, but I can't give you much more information. I care about Mason too much to break his confidence," I told Hudson regretfully.

Maybe I thought that Hudson and Mason would probably get along, and I was a true believer that you could never have enough family at your back since I had none myself. But the ultimate decision of whether or not Mason wanted to communicate with his cousins was completely his call.

Hudson's grin returned, and I had to admit that it made him even more handsome than he already was. "I think we'd all like to be invited to the wedding," he said teasingly.

"What wedding?" I frowned at him.

"Yours and Mason's," Hudson replied as his smile got broader. "Come on, Laura. No man is going to spill his guts to a woman unless he plans on marrying her. He's obviously told you more than he's told his siblings."

"Still trying to drag more personal information out of me?" I asked. "I hate to burst your bubble, but Mason and I have no plans of getting married. We're just…seeing each other."

Even if I wanted to, I couldn't explain why Mason had told me the truth when he hadn't even told his siblings. It was way too personal.

"He trusts you," Hudson observed. "And with good reason, I might add. Trying to get any significant information out of you is nearly impossible, much to my dismay."

"I'd never betray Mason," I said in a warning voice. "Ever."

He nodded with what looked like approval as he answered, "I respect that. Then we can change the subject. Tell me about your business. I'm interested."

I let out a sigh of relief that we could discuss something else, but I never got a word out of my mouth about Perfect Harmony.

I heard a stuttering sound that sounded like gunfire, and then I was immediately struck with a searing pain to my right side.

I watched in horror as Hudson reached inside his suit jacket and pulled out a handgun. He rocketed out of his chair and tackled me to the floor, his body covering mine as the popping sound continued for what seemed like an eternity.

Somebody is shooting up the restaurant!

"Stay down," Hudson growled. "Don't fucking move a muscle."

I wasn't going anywhere with Hudson's weight on top of me, but I had no plans of balking at his order in the first place.

My breathing was ragged and painful, and the whole room was spinning.

My body started to shake beneath his bulk, and I suddenly thought that I wished I had told Mason that I loved him.

By the sounds of the mass panic and screams all around me, and the continuous shots coming from a weapon, I was pretty sure I'd never have the chance to tell him in the future.

"Fuck!" I heard Hudson's angry hiss. I knew he'd been hit. I'd heard an inflection of pain in his voice.

One moment, my mind was racing, trying to figure out if there was anything I could do to help Hudson.

And then, in a heartbeat, everything went dark.

Chapter 19

Mason

"She's only been gone for five days, and I feel like it's been a year," I complained to Carter as we sat in my office on Friday afternoon.

He shot me a knowing grin. "She's back Sunday night, right?"

"Yeah, so don't expect me in the office until late on Monday," I warned him.

"Bro, you look so damn miserable that I think you should take Monday off."

"I might," I answered irritably.

Jesus! I'd played every damn mind game I could think of to take my thoughts away from Laura. Not one of them had worked.

"You'll live," Carter said with an amused chortle. "It just doesn't feel like you're going to right now."

I glared at him. "Easy for you to say. You know that Brynn will be there when you get home."

"She *was* gone a week ago," he reminded me. "So I know how you feel. And I have to say I'm glad she's done modeling."

"You talk her into that?" I asked suspiciously.

"Oh, hell, no," Carter replied. "In the end, I want Brynn to be happy. It was her decision. How about Laura?"

"Her decision, too. I wouldn't want to see her do something she doesn't want or isn't ready to do."

Carter looked down at his cell phone as he said, "It's funny that their independence is one of the things we love about both of them, but it's one of the hardest things for us to accept."

"It isn't that I *can't* accept it," I told Carter, my tone thoughtful. "I just don't want to see her get hurt. If she could go anywhere she wanted to go without the danger of some crazy bastard causing her harm, I'd be fucking happy to suffer through that time without her if she was happy. But I have a lot of enemies, Carter. Too many. We didn't make it to the top without sending some companies under, or killing off their business. Money is a big motivator when it comes to crazies. It isn't like we haven't had people make serious threats to us in the past."

Carter nodded as he scrolled through his phone. "Yeah. I get it. And you get more of those than anyone because you do the heavy lifting on the business end."

I watched him, knowing I didn't have his full attention. Unlike some people, it wasn't like Carter to have his face buried in his phone while he was having a discussion. "What are you doing?"

He looked up immediately. "Looking at a breaking news story about one of those crazies we were talking about," he said carefully. "I'm still trying to figure out what happened. Some asshole went into a San Diego restaurant and started shooting with a modified assault rifle."

"Where in San Diego?" I asked him, telling myself that it could have been anywhere.

"Close to downtown," he said absently as he continued to look at news articles. "Two people died, and there's a lot of wounded."

"What else do you see? I mean, what are the chances that Laura was anywhere near there?"

San Diego was a large city, and chances were that Laura was somewhere else. I'd texted with her earlier in the morning, and she'd said she had a couple of business meetings.

I pulled my phone out of my pocket to see if there were any messages that I hadn't seen.

Nothing from her since morning.

I quickly sent her a text to let me know she was okay because I'd heard about the shooting.

"Are you texting Laura?" Carter asked.

"Yeah. I just want to make sure she was far away from that location."

Carter looked up at me, his expression grim. "Jesus! I don't want to tell you this..."

There was a sinking feeling in the pit of my gut as I saw his expression.

Carter wasn't an alarmist, so the tension on his face was fucking terrifying.

"What?" I said in an edgy voice. "Just tell me."

Carter stood and walked to my desk. "Laura *was* there. Apparently with Hudson Montgomery, although how the hell she knows him escapes me. Maybe they're friends?"

Hudson Montgomery?

Why in the fuck would she be in a restaurant with *him?*

"The reporting has to be wrong. She doesn't know him. She never mentioned seeing him while she was in San Diego."

"It's not wrong," Carter said solemnly as he put his phone right in front of me. "That's her picture with him that was taken by a reporter for the gossip columns right before the shooting started. They stalk all the Montgomery brothers. I guess they got a photo of the two of them together before the chaos started. The reporter survived, and they just broke the picture with the story. Hudson Montgomery *was* there with Laura. I don't know why they were together, but I am sure it was totally innocent."

I stared at the photo in front of me, enlarged to full screen by Carter.

It *was* Laura and Hudson Montgomery.

Their hands were touching, and they looked like they were in some kind of serious discussion. There was no smile on Laura's face, which was highly unusual for a woman who was as upbeat as she was.

"What the fuck," I growled, and then slammed my hand down on my desk so hard it was fucking painful.

"We need to find out what happened, Mason. Don't jump to conclusions until we have the facts. We need to know if Laura is okay," Carter said calmly as he took his phone back. "Let me make some calls."

I stood up, trying to get my head together. "I'm heading there *now*," I told him. "Let me know what you find out. I need the jet ready to fly."

"Did your jet come back to home base after dropping Laura off?"

I nodded. "It's here."

"I'll call the crew. Mason, try not to jump to any conclusions about Laura and Hudson. She's not interested in him."

"Fuck that!" I growled. "I just need to know that Laura is okay. That she's alive and well. I can deal with Montgomery later. Hell, I trust *her*. I just don't trust *him*."

Carter nodded. "I'll hold down the fort here since Jett isn't around, and I'll call some people and find out anything I can. You know we aren't going to get much from general news reports. I'll call you once you're in flight," Carter said as he followed me out of the office door.

"I'm heading straight to the airport," I told him as we stopped in front of the express elevator.

I raked a hand through my hair, trying not to think about Laura being anything other than unharmed, while Carter called my flight crew to make sure they'd be ready to take off.

"Did they say who died?" I asked Carter after he hung up. Part of me didn't want to know, but I needed *something* to keep me from losing it.

We were stepping into the elevator as Carter kept flipping through stuff on his phone. "One male, one female. No other info."

Holy! Fucking! Shit!

I ignored the way my heart was hammering, and the chest pain that was tearing through my sternum.

Carter gave me a supportive clap on the back as we stepped out of the elevator. "She'll be okay, bro. We have to keep believing that until we find out otherwise," Carter said hoarsely.

"I have no damn choice *but* to believe that. Any other outcome is unacceptable," I rumbled as we walked through the lobby.

"Brynn is going to be worried sick. And she's going to want to talk to Laura. So keep me posted," Carter insisted.

"I will," I replied absently, my mind already focused on figuring out what in the hell had happened in San Diego a few hours ago.

Carter and I parted when we got to our designated parking spaces.

I knew he was headed back to his house to talk to Brynn, and to dig up any information he could find.

I broke nearly every traffic law in existence on my way to the airport.

I was in the air and headed south within an hour to see if I was going to stay relatively sane, or if my entire world was going to come crashing down on my head.

Chapter 20

Laura

When I opened my eyes, everything seemed blurred and tilted in my world.

What in the hell?

I couldn't make sense of where I was or what had happened. All I knew was that my chest was heavy, like I was trying to breathe, but couldn't, because there was an elephant sitting on my chest.

I need to get up. I need to get out of bed.

I *had* to be home, but nothing looked like my condo or Mason's house.

The second I moved, I gasped as a pain so excruciating ripped through my upper body that it forced me to lay back down.

"Don't move," I heard a familiar baritone voice say insistently.

"Mason?" I said, barely getting a whisper out of my mouth.

"It's Hudson," the voice explained. "You just came out of surgery. But from what I gathered when I called Mason's office, he'll be here soon. His assistant said he was on his way to San Diego. Just relax."

Hudson?

Hudson Montgomery.

Suddenly, I remembered everything.

The gunshots.

The terror.

The pain.

And then…nothing.

I turned my head carefully, and I could see Hudson standing right next to the bed.

"I'm in the hospital? What happened?"

"You don't remember?" Hudson asked.

"Not much. I assume I was shot. But you were shot, too." I looked at him, alarmed.

"Mine was nothing. Just a graze. They stitched me up in the emergency department. I'm fine, Laura, but you caught a bullet. Luckily, it didn't hit a rib, but it did puncture your lung. You have a chest tube in right now. They took you to surgery to explore the wound and close it properly. But the chest tube has to stay in for a while. I'm sorry. I wish I could have seen the bastard coming," he finished, his tone angry and remorseful at the same time.

I could remember Hudson hurtling toward me, and taking me to the ground. "Don't be sorry," I whispered. "You probably saved my life. I thought I was dying. What happened to everyone else in the restaurant?"

"There were two fatalities. The shooter was a disgruntled former employee. He killed the two owners in the kitchen and then started to shoot indiscriminately everywhere else," he said stoically.

Tears sprang to my eyes because two people had been killed so senselessly. "Did they catch him?"

"I killed him," Hudson answered without an ounce of remorse in his voice. "There were other injuries, but it sounds like they'll all survive."

I vaguely remembered that Hudson had pulled out a gun, but I didn't know he'd shot the perpetrator.

"Thank God," I said in a choked voice, barely able to contain my urge to openly sob from the entire ordeal.

I felt Hudson's hand stroking my hair. "Don't cry. It will hurt like hell."

I nodded my head. "I know. Any kind of movement hurts."

"You're going to be okay, Laura. It will take time to heal. You're in intensive care right now, but the nurse said you'll be able to go to the surgical floor once the chest tube gets removed and you're more stable." He pulled up a chair, sat by the bed, and then reached for my hand.

I took it. I felt like I needed something or someone to hang on to, and Hudson had protected me with his own body. I didn't know what would have happened if he hadn't gotten me down to the ground. "Thank you," I croaked out hoarsely.

"Don't thank me," he said huskily. "I'm just glad you're going to live through all this. I won't even try to pretend that it will be easy. It was a pretty traumatic event."

"Luckily, I was unconscious for most of it," I explained. "The last thing I remember is you telling me not to move. After that, everything is pretty much a blank."

"It might be better that way," he considered. "Not the getting shot part, but the unconscious part. The carnage wasn't pretty."

Sadness overwhelmed me, and I couldn't help but wonder how the other victims were faring, and how the family of the two restaurant owners were going to cope with the violent death of their loved ones.

I hurt, but I'd be okay.

I had no idea what was going to happen to everyone else.

Hudson squeezed my hand. "Hey, don't overthink all of this right now. It will make you crazy. Just concentrate on getting well."

At the moment, I felt weak and fragile, so being healthy and whole again seemed like a difficult stretch.

"Where did you get hit?" I asked Hudson.

"My shoulder," he answered. "But it's all patched up."

He didn't look like he was in pain. He just looked…weary. "Why in the world were you carrying a gun?"

I was fairly certain it wasn't easy to get a concealed carry permit in San Diego.

"That's a discussion for another day. Long story," Hudson said lightly.

"I think I have nothing but time right now. And I'd definitely be a captive audience."

I'd be happy to hear Hudson talk. Anything to get my mind off what had happened earlier in the day.

Unfortunately, I knew I wasn't going to get the story as I saw Hudson's eyes go to the doorway of my hospital room.

"Laura, you have another visitor," the nurse said with a soft, soothing voice as she entered.

Hudson's mouth formed into a wry smile as he stood. "I bet I can guess who it is."

"Mason," I said longingly. God, I hoped it was him. I desperately needed to see him right now.

Hudson let go of my hand. "I'll go let him come in. They only want short visits, and one person at a time right now. I'll come back in tomorrow. Get some rest, Laura."

"Since he's not a relative, I couldn't give him any information," the nurse explained.

"I'll fill him in," Hudson told me.

I nodded. "Take care of yourself. Even though you're making it sound like no big deal, you have to be hurting."

He shrugged, and then winced, obviously forgetting that he had a wound in his shoulder. "I'll live. I've survived worse," he said ruefully before he strode toward the door.

I watched him leave, hoping he wasn't in more pain than he'd let on.

Hudson Montgomery had saved my life, and I knew we'd always have a bond because of the horrific experience we'd shared.

Eventually, I'd get the truth out of him as to why he carried a weapon, and why he had such lightning-fast reactions, even while he was in the middle of chaos.

There was way more to Hudson Montgomery than he was willing to share.

I'd seen a very quick glimpse of somebody way different than his public persona.

Somebody dark and heroic, which made me wonder exactly how many secrets Hudson *really* had.

Chapter 21

Mason

The moment that Hudson Montgomery came into the empty waiting room, I grabbed the bastard and pinned him against the wall. "What in the hell did you do to her?" I growled.

"Fuck. I'm injured, man. Let go," he said with an agitated groan.

I could see the pain in his eyes, and even though I wanted to kill him, I knew I wouldn't.

I let go.

"You better explain yourself pretty damn quick," I warned. "I want to know what happened, why it happened, why you were with my woman, and if she's okay. Answer the last question first. Is she okay? The medical staff won't tell me shit."

Hudson moved away from the wall. "She was shot. The bullet went between her ribs, but it did hit her lung bad enough for it to deflate. She had to have surgery, but yes, she's going to be okay. However, the last thing she needs is your bullshit. Get a fucking grip before you go in there. She's been through a really traumatic experience, and she nearly died. What she needs right now is a man who has his shit together. This isn't about you. Remember that."

Fuck! I wanted to punch the bastard out, but I didn't want to get booted out of the hospital. Plus, somewhere in my rational mind, I knew he was right.

I pulled my phone out of my pocket. "This is being broadcasted all over the internet," I informed him as I turned the phone so he could see the photo of him and Laura.

"Shit!" he exclaimed angrily. "Yes, we were together, because I asked her for a meeting while she was here. I led her to believe that it was about business. And we weren't touching each other like it looks in the picture. I was handing her my business card to give to *you*. I knew you two were close, and I was hoping she might be able to tell me exactly why your ornery ass never returns my calls. Don't put this on her. It's all on me. And I hate myself for putting her in that position. If I hadn't asked her to meet me, she wouldn't be in intensive care. If you want to be angry at somebody, be pissed off at *me*, not her."

I could see the guilt he was feeling written all over his face, and although I didn't feel the least bit sorry for the bastard, I did start to calm down.

"I'm not angry at Laura. It wasn't her fault. How bad are her injuries?. Really?" I asked huskily.

"Bad," he answered. "But not fatal. It's going to take her time to recover from it. She's hurting right now, physically and emotionally. Just support her, Mason. That's what she needs right now."

"Of course I'm going to support her," I snarled back at him.

"For what it's worth, she's an amazing woman. She has your back, cousin. When it comes to you, she's very tight-lipped, and incredibly loyal. She cares about you, man. A lot."

Most of my animosity toward Hudson was fading away. "How are you doing? You said you're hurt."

"My graze to the shoulder is nothing compared to what Laura is going through. I'll heal a hell of a lot faster than she will," he said.

"Why did this happen?" I asked.

"As to the what and why part of your questions, the *why* is senseless. The perp was a disgruntled employee who got fired because he didn't show up for work half the time. *What* happened? The bastard shot the restaurant owners who fired him first, and then started to shoot up the entire place. He was a lunatic," Hudson informed me in a brusque tone that contained more than a little acrimony.

"I'll kill the bastard," I growled.

"I'd love to give you that privilege, but I had to do it myself, so he didn't kill more people in that restaurant," Hudson said solemnly. "I shot him. It was a kill shot."

What the fuck?

"Do I even want to know why you had a concealed weapon in a crowded restaurant in downtown San Diego?" I grumbled.

Maybe I didn't know Hudson, but he was my damn cousin by blood. He wasn't the intended target of this shooting, but did he have enemies who wanted to kill him so much that he had to carry a loaded weapon on him all the time?

"I have a permit to carry," Hudson said with a wry smile. "I'm not into the mafia or drug running. Everything surrounding Montgomery Mining is perfectly legit."

"It's not easy to get a concealed carry permit in this state," I reminded him. "You need to have good cause to carry. So what I the hell are you into?"

"Let's leave the explanation for another time," Hudson suggested. "It's a long story. And I have to get to the police station to give them my statement."

"I need to see Laura," I said, my jaw clenched tightly now that I knew exactly how one asshole had hurt so damn many people.

"She knows you're here. Go. There's nobody in her room now, and I think she'll feel better after she sees you. She needs to rest, and I think all of the shit that happened is just starting to hit her right now." Hudson stepped back to get out of the doorway.

Hudson added, "If you need a place to stay, I can put you up at my place."

I shook my head. "I want to stay with Laura."

"If they kick you out, call me," Hudson said as he exited the waiting room.

My cousin was forgotten the moment he left, and I picked up the internal phone to get buzzed into the intensive care unit.

The nurse inside the door directed me to Laura's room, and I stopped at the door the moment I saw her lying in a hospital bed, looking so damn fragile and connected to so many tubes and wires that she appeared to be even more frail than she probably was in reality.

I pushed myself to walk into the room, and forget about how damn angry I was that she was in this condition, because Hudson was right.

I had to forget about my own damn fears about losing her.

This was all about Laura right now.

It wasn't about me.

I felt like I'd been sucker-punched when she shot me a weak smile as she saw me approaching the bed.

Her voice was weak as she mumbled, "I'd love to throw myself into your arms right now, but I'm a little tied down by all this medical stuff."

It was meant to be a joke, but I couldn't manage to put even a small smile on my face.

I leaned down and stroked her beautiful hair, which looked matted and lifeless. "I was fucking afraid that you were dead," I said in a choked voice that I barely recognized as my own.

A tear trickled from the corner of her eye. "I know. I'm sorry."

"It's not your damn fault," I said tightly. "You were just having lunch, for fuck's sake."

"I'm still sorry that you had to worry about this. I'm going to be fine, Mason."

Did she really think there would *ever* be a time when I wouldn't be frantic about her safety?

Dammit! After this incident, I was going to have a hard time letting her leave my sight.

Really, this was my fault. I should have just answered Hudson's calls and told him to fuck off. Or maybe we could have just had a casual relationship, so he wouldn't have reached out to other people I cared about to try to get to me.

Problem was, I hadn't wanted to talk to him.

I *had* a family.

I didn't need more, especially not family members I hadn't even known existed.

When Hudson had first reached out to me, I'd been floored that I was blood-related to the Montgomery family. My mother had never mentioned exactly who had assaulted her.

After that, I decided I just didn't give a damn because I already had all the family I needed. *Real* family who knew me and gave a damn about me. I didn't want cousins who weren't cousins to my brothers and sisters, too.

I would have needed to tell my siblings the truth, and I didn't want to be *different*.

However, my own stubbornness had eventually affected Laura in a way that was physically and emotionally devastating.

Right now, I hated being the person who had caused this to happen to her.

Laura shouldn't have been in that restaurant. She *wouldn't* have been if it wasn't for me being in her life.

Hudson would have never contacted her.

And she wouldn't be here in this hospital bed, looking like she'd barely survived a horrific mass shooting.

I leaned down and kissed her forehead, and then swiped away the offending tear on the side of her face.

"I'm so glad you're here now," she whispered.

"I'm not going anywhere," I promised. "Sleep, Laura. Don't try to talk. Hudson told me everything. Just rest. I'll be here when you wake up."

I was fucking going to be glued to her side until she was one hundred percent healed.

After that, I was going to do whatever the hell it took to make sure she'd never go through something like this again.

Her eyes started to flutter closed, and she answered, "Just one thing I have to tell you first. When I was hurt and not sure I was going to live through the shooting, I regretted not saying it before."

"What?" I asked, my voice husky with emotion.

"I love you, Mason. I want you to know that because I don't want to ever regret not telling you again," she said, right before she sighed and fell asleep.

Chapter 22

Laura

It took almost a month after my injury before I felt completely normal again.

Unfortunately, rather than bringing us closer, my whole recovery period had seemed to make Mason more distant than he'd ever been before.

Oh, he was there for every single need I'd had until just recently. He'd been incredibly supportive, pushing me and keeping my spirits up when things got difficult. But he did it from an emotional distance.

Until I was completely healed.

Now, I hadn't heard from him *at all* for several days. He was making every excuse in the world to avoid me.

If I called his cell phone or texted, I got no reply.

If I called his office, I got some excuse from his secretary, who I talked to more than I talked to him these days.

He was working.

He was in a meeting.

He was out for lunch.

He was just…unavailable. I think his secretary used that one when she just didn't know what in the hell to say.

There was something wrong.

I could sense it.

I'd been feeling pretty good after the first two weeks, yet there had been no intimacy between Mason and me at all.

Oh, he'd said all the right words, but he'd been…emotionally vacant.

The man didn't kiss me except for a quick peck on the lips, or even worse, my cheek or forehead, like I was a child and not a woman he supposedly wanted to be in an exclusive relationship with.

Mason treated me more like a close friend than as a significant other.

"Maybe he thinks you're still recovering," Brynn suggested as we had coffee and pieces of cake she'd stopped for at my favorite bakery before she'd arrived at my condo around lunchtime.

We were seated at the small table in my kitchen. Brynn and I had been meeting somewhere every single day, trying to catch up on the time and events we'd lost while I'd been getting my health back.

Brynn had been there for me, too, whenever I needed her. But most of our discussions had revolved around my health during the first few weeks of my recovery.

I shook my head. "He knows I have a clean bill of health. He was at the doctor's office with me last week when she told me I didn't have to come back again unless I had any complications, which she didn't expect would happen."

"You *are* back to your full exercise routine," Brynn observed. "You look fantastic."

"I'm doing even *more* than I was before," I said. "Since I'm not as strict on my diet now, I walk a lot to keep fit and healthy."

"Okay," Brynn conceded. "His behavior is…weird. No sex at all?"

"Nada," I confirmed after I'd swallowed a bite of my cake. "He won't even really kiss me. I can't put a finger on it, Brynn. He's been so supportive, and with me every step of the way during my recovery. But it's like part of him is…gone. He treats me more like a friend than a lover. I think maybe he just lost his romantic interest."

It was the first time I'd actually said that thought aloud, and speaking my conclusion hurt like hell. Unfortunately, as I'd gone through the last few days of his complete absence, I had to be honest with myself.

Mason doesn't want me anymore.

"No way," Brynn denied. "The man is crazy about you."

"I told him I loved him right after the shooting happened. He never even acknowledged it. It's like I never said it. Maybe it was just too soon. But I couldn't help myself. I almost died, and I wanted him to know the truth."

It had nearly killed me that he'd never said it back. Not once. Nor had he even reminded me that I'd said it.

Obviously, he hadn't wanted to hear it again.

"Have you talked to your counselor about it?" Brynn asked.

"Not really. She's more of an expert at dealing with PTSD." It had been Mason who had insisted on getting me counseling after the incident. I'd mentioned to him that I'd had nightmares about it, and he'd insisted that I get a counselor to work through the emotional part of the trauma.

It had definitely helped.

"Maybe Mason is still afraid that he'll hurt you," Brynn pondered.

"Doubtful," I replied. "He knows I'm strong. I worked out in his home gym with him almost every day until he stopped inviting me a couple of days ago. But I do have a lot of scars. And he's seen gross things that no boyfriend should see during the early part of a relationship. Taking out the chest tube was excruciating and messy, and I haven't exactly looked normal until recently. I was pretty weak and beaten down for a while there. He was there for *all* of that. Maybe he just looks at me differently now."

"If that's true, which I doubt it is, then he isn't the man I think he is," Brynn answered in a disappointed tone. "A guy who really loves you is going to eventually see your weaker times. Your sick times. And they're going to go through childbirth with you, which is pretty damn bloody. Never in a million years would I have said that Mason was that shallow."

"It was a long recovery," I reminded her. "It wasn't exactly like I had a flu virus for four or five days."

"Pregnancy lasts for *nine months*, and then there's the birth itself," she retorted. "You were the one really hurting."

"He never claimed to love me," I told her.

"He does," Brynn said emphatically. "Carter said Mason nearly lost it when he found out you were in that restaurant."

"Well, he's avoiding me *now*. He even missed our Sunday call. He hasn't called or texted in three days now. And all during my recovery, he's treated me like a sister or a friend. He's obviously letting go now that I'm healed." I tried not to let my hurt and frustration surface, but my eyes welled up with tears anyway.

"Don't give up, Laura. I don't know what's going through his head right now, but I don't believe he sees you as a friend or a sister."

"We haven't slept in the same bed since my injury," I confessed. "He stayed at his house, and I stayed in my condo. He was always gone by nighttime. Even when I was too weak to be really intimate with him, he could have just…stayed."

Brynn was silent for a moment before she answered, "I have to admit, I can't explain that. You did say he was there for your birthday, though."

I rolled my eyes. "Yes, he was there. He brought takeout and a cake. We watched movies all evening. In separate reclining chairs. He gave me a gift card as a birthday present. It wasn't exactly a romance filled evening."

"Agreed," Brynn said glumly. "I don't know what the hell is wrong with him."

"He obviously wants out," I said, my voice sadder than I wanted it to be. "What I don't get is why he didn't tell me instead of avoiding my calls. But I'm getting the message loud and clear. I'm not calling or texting him anymore."

"What about Hudson?" Brynn said gently. "He's been flying in a lot to see you."

I shrugged. "He's nothing more than a friend. Hudson is easy to talk to, but I'm not attracted to him that way, and he's not into me that way, either. We just…talk. He's kind of like the brother I never had."

Brynn snorted. "I never thought I'd hear a single woman say that about one of the Montgomery brothers. From the few times I've met Hudson, I thought he was a pretty nice guy. And it's fantastic that he's interested in Perfect Harmony."

I cringed just a little. I hated the fact that I hadn't been able to tell Brynn exactly why I knew Hudson. And I never would, no matter what happened between Mason and me in the future. Until Mason changed his mind about telling his siblings the truth about him being adopted, I'd be sticking to my story that I met Hudson for a meeting about Perfect Harmony when the shooting had occurred.

Hudson had done the same, and wouldn't be informing anybody about the relationship between himself and Mason unless the truth came out.

For now, Hudson seemed perfectly content with keeping the secret.

Over the last month, I'd come to value Hudson's friendship. He had flown into Seattle often to see how I was doing those first couple of weeks. He'd completely healed from his own injury quickly, and I was totally well again, but he continued to call me at least twice a week.

"Hudson isn't investing in Perfect Harmony, but he's there any time I need business advice," I shared. "He's a powerful business ally, but I mostly just appreciate him being a friend."

Hudson and I spoke about what had happened that horrible day in the restaurant, but we'd also moved on to other topics.

I'd shared some of my past as a foster kid.

He'd shared some of his family history.

We'd bonded over the fact that we'd both had a pretty dysfunctional childhood.

I'd concluded that there was a lot more to the man than what I'd read about him in the past.

The only time he'd really shut me down was when I'd asked him about why he'd been carrying a gun in the restaurant. All he'd said was that he had his reasons, and he'd asked me to trust him that it wasn't for any nefarious purposes.

He hadn't wanted to talk about it, and I hadn't wanted to push him to discuss something that was probably none of my business anyway, so I'd done exactly what he'd asked me to do. I trusted him. I had no reason not to. The man had probably saved my life.

"So what are you going to do about Mason?" Brynn asked softly.

I shrugged. "What can I do? I can't make him love me. I haven't called him lately because he doesn't return my calls. It's over, Brynn. I'm not going to keep torturing myself."

I tried not to get too heavy with Brynn since she was married to Mason's brother. The last thing I wanted to do was cause family friction of any kind, but it was really difficult to hold back. Brynn was my best friend, and I felt like my heart had been fractured into a million tiny little pieces.

"I think you should force him to at least give you a reason why he's backed off."

My heart ached as I told her, "It doesn't really matter why. And I think his reason is perfectly obvious. The interest isn't there anymore. If it was, we'd still be seeing each other."

God, I missed the intimacy that Mason and I had shared. I still wanted to be close to him so badly that it hurt, even though he obviously didn't share my compulsion.

I got up to make another cup of coffee, and Brynn grabbed her empty mug to do the same.

I turned my back so she wouldn't see the tears flowing down my cheeks.

"Hey, he'll come around. Mason might be stubborn, but he isn't stupid," Brynn said gently.

"I'll survive," I said as I put my mug under the coffeemaker, put a pod into it, and slammed the top closed. "I got through being shot—I think I can get over a guy who doesn't want me anymore." I pushed the button for the coffee to brew.

"Laura, Mason isn't like the previous men in your life. You're *really* in love with him. I know you're hurting, even though you haven't said a word about how badly he's hurt you. But I know. You're my best friend," Brynn said in a sympathetic voice.

She pulled on my upper arm with minimal pressure, urging me to turn to her.

Finally, I faced her with a sob. "It's killing me, Brynn. I don't know what to do. The Mason I knew is gone, and I miss him so damn much."

I'd thought I could put on my big girl panties and handle what was happening between Mason and me, deal with it like a strong woman should.

I was wrong.

I threw myself into Brynn's arms and wept.

Chapter 23

Mason

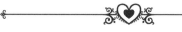

Laura Hastings Blog Entry, Today, 9:30 a.m.

I want to thank you all for your support during the time that I was recovering from my injuries. I know it's been awhile since I've done a blog post, even though I've been completely healed for over a week now.

Unfortunately, I've been going through a different kind of pain now, and I guess I just didn't feel like I had much to talk about.

But I do now.

I think every woman has been through a relationship where it was hard to let go. Well, I've been having a difficult time doing that myself, but now, I think it's time for me to move on.

You see, sometimes I think difficult circumstances can make or break a relationship. You either form a bond that's even closer than it was before, or that tragedy rips you apart because that bond was never strong enough to hold through adversity in the first place.

In my case, the relationship didn't stand the test. I couldn't make somebody love me who really didn't.

At first, I blamed myself, my scars, my weakness during a really down period in my life. But guess what…in real life, there are going to be times that are hard in many different ways. And if your love isn't strong enough on both sides, that relationship will collapse.

It will hurt.

There will be tears and pain.

You'll feel so damn lonely that it's physically painful for a while.

My advice? Stand back and let that relationship fall. Don't try to hold onto something that isn't worth saving. I'm not saying it's easy, but trying to grasp on to something that isn't real is even more painful.

Ladies, we all deserve better.

We have to find that partner who will stay, even when your whole world is falling apart.

Is it going to hurt? Hell, yes. In fact, you are going to have moments when you never want to try again, and those emotional wounds are so excruciating that you completely fall apart.

Mourn it. Own it. But decide when it's time to move on and just admit that the relationship wasn't what you'd thought it would be.

Then, find a person who is going to love you…no matter what happens in your life, physical and emotional scars and all.

Those partners are out there.

Sometimes you just need to kiss a lot of frogs to find your Prince Charming. :)

Eventually, I'll kiss a few more frogs myself, and hope for the best.

Smile at yourself in the mirror at least once today. You're beautiful, whether you know it or not.

Xoxoxo ~ Laura

"What in the fuck did you do?" Hudson Montgomery asked angrily as he walked through my office door.

"By all means, come in," I said sarcastically, annoyed that the man had found a way into the executive offices, and on a damn weekend, too.

Not that I even bothered to question *how* that breach had happened.

Knowing what I did about Hudson now, I had no doubt he could find his way in through any kind of security.

"Did you read her fucking blog?" Hudson grumbled in a furious tone as he took a chair across from my desk. "I could feel her pain radiating through the damn computer, no matter how much she talked about healing, and I don't like it. Laura has become like a second sister to me, and you're a dumbass. She's probably the best thing that ever happened to you. Did you just blow her off?"

"I was avoiding her calls for a few days. But I talked to her on the phone yesterday. I called her because I knew we needed some kind of closure," I admitted. "I told her that I didn't think we could continue our relationship. It wasn't like she argued about it."

Granted, I hadn't explained myself, either, so I had probably deserved her cold goodbye before she'd hung up on me.

"Did you fucking expect her to argue with you? You've treated her like shit since she got well. She told me you ignored her calls, and pretty much just disappeared." Hudson sounded furious. "I didn't interfere then. I figured you'd come to your senses. But when I read that blog this morning, it ripped my damn heart out. What in the hell are you doing, Mason? I know damn well that you love her."

It had torn my heart to shreds, too, but I didn't want to admit that to Hudson. He'd never understand what I had to do.

My cousin and I had finally decided to make peace, and we spoke occasionally, mostly on the phone. I couldn't say we were friends. More like friendly adversaries.

He'd openly shared every part of his life, and I had to admit that I had a reluctant respect for the guy and his brothers because of some of the things I'd discovered that weren't general knowledge.

I'd shared almost nothing with him, and since I still hadn't shared the truth with my siblings, his brothers and his sister still didn't even know I existed.

Which was fine with me.

Most of the time.

"My relationship with Laura is over," I said stoically. "It has been since the day she nearly died because of me."

"Because of *me*," he corrected. "I'm the one who invited her to that restaurant."

I raised a brow. "You forget that you only did that to reach *me*."

"This is a ridiculous conversation," he exploded. "Are you really willing to let go of a woman who loves you that damn much? Some of us might be nasty and ornery, but we've never had a *stupid* Montgomery in the whole lot of us."

"I'm a Lawson," I growled.

"You're both," he shot back. "And I asked you if you've read her blog post."

"I did," I said sharply.

"You hurt her, and I'd like to beat the shit out of you until you hurt just as much as she does. She doesn't deserve this from you, Mason. Especially considering that you love her just as much as she loves you."

I lost it as I slammed my hand down on the desk so hard the whole thing rattled. "Yes, *dammit!* I will let her go if that means she'll be safe and happy for the rest of her life. Sometimes, love has to be stronger than the desire to be with somebody. It has to be strong enough to let go to fucking protect the person you love. Do you honestly think it was easy for me to watch Laura go through all that physical pain? Or the emotional pain from the trauma? It nearly killed me, and I love her so damn much that I can't watch it ever happen again. If she's with me, she's always going to be a target for some lunatic to come and do it again, or worse. And she's independent enough to want some freedom. Hell, I probably wouldn't have ever let her go anywhere alone, without me there. I *can't* put her in prison that way. I can't." My voice was hoarse with emotion that I couldn't contain.

Hudson gaped at me. "So this is all some self-sacrificing bullshit? You're trying to protect her?"

"Why the hell else would I do it?" I said, my chest heaving. "As long as she's attached to me, she's going to be a target for every person I've ever ruined in the past. I get death threats on a regular basis. I'd rather let her go than to know that I hurt her in any damn way."

The day that Laura had told me that she loved me was the best and the worst day of my life.

At that moment, the second that the words had left her mouth, I'd known what I was going to have to do to protect her.

"Did you ever bother to give her that choice? Did you offer her a compromise? I get that you want to protect her. Hell, I want to protect her. But that doesn't mean that you both have to walk around like zombies forever because your hearts are fucking broken. That's crazy, Mason. You do love her, right?"

I shot him a murderous look. "I just said that I did. Too damn much. I haven't been worth a shit to anybody since the day you two were shot. And no, we didn't *discuss* the fact that she wasn't safe as long as she was with me. There is no damn compromise. She's either a target with me, or safe being away from me."

"You do look like hell," he considered. "But here's the thing…safety is never a guarantee. Shit happens in life, no matter how cautious you might be. Either one us could get killed in a plane crash, or even crossing the street. You can't protect her from everything bad in life."

"And *that* drove me fucking crazy," I growled. "I *should* be able to protect her. But I didn't. I wanted her to be happy, so I agreed to not have a tail on her in San Diego."

"A security detail wouldn't have helped," Hudson said solemnly. "It happened too damn fast. I was sitting right there with her, and I couldn't prevent her from getting shot. So don't blame yourself for that."

I raked a hand through my hair. "I can't help it."

"Forget the shooting. It's over. *You* hurt her this time. Badly," he said accusingly.

"Then what in the hell would you have me do?"

He hesitated before he said, "Negotiate. Or just tell her that for your peace of mind, you need a detail on her until you feel a little more relaxed. The shooting was a once-in-a-lifetime thing, Mason. The odds of it ever happening again are astronomical. Really, it wasn't your fault or mine. It was because some madman shot up a restaurant. You're giving up your whole damn life out of the fear of seeing Laura hurt that way again. Did it ever occur to you that her *not* being with you makes her even less safe? You know you're going to take care of her the best you can. And time together with no further problems would have helped you get over this crippling fear. Right now, she's alone. Maybe she isn't a target of your enemies, but there are other crazy people out there."

"I don't think I'll ever get over it. She'd end up a with a tail for the rest of her life" I said gruffly. "And she's being protected. I have guys on her ass. I just asked them to keep their distance and be discreet."

"And how long will that go on?"

"Until everybody realizes that we aren't seeing each other. At all. Or maybe until I feel like she'll be okay."

"What happens if she's stalked by a mentally ill fan of hers, or she ends up with some asshole who beats her up, or abuses her? What happens when she chooses someone who wouldn't protect her or treat her as well as you would?"

I hesitated. "I'll kill him."

Hudson shrugged. "You wouldn't even know it's happening. It could be a year down the road or more. I think right now, she's pretty much hung up on your dumb ass, no matter how much she talks about moving on. But she did mention that she'd eventually kiss a few frogs again. She'll date somebody else eventually."

Christ! I hadn't really thought about what could happen if Laura started dating again. Probably because I couldn't stand the thought of any other guy touching her. Ever.

She's. Mine.

Laura was always meant to be mine.

"Are you starting to re-think this whole 'getting out of her life' scenario?" Hudson asked mildly.

"No," I said, but my conviction wasn't as strong.

He was right. I *would* be there for Laura. Someone else…*might not.*

Hudson crossed his arms over his chest. "So how would you feel if I decided I might want to make my relationship with Laura into something more? She's a beautiful, compassionate, caring, intelligent woman. I already care about her."

I shot him a wild-eyed look. *Was Hudson fucking with me? Or was he serious?* "I'd kill you," I concluded.

He smirked. "Not liking the thought of anyone else touching her? Well, you better get over it, because she's eventually going to end up with somebody else. She has way too much to offer to a man to stay single forever."

He *was* screwing with me, and I sure as hell didn't appreciate it. "Bastard," I rasped.

"I'm just trying to make you see reality, man. You have a choice to make, and I'm not certain it's actually not too damn late for that, but you either throw her to the wolves, who may or may not be good to her, or you take the risk and make damn sure you do everything you can to make her happy and safe."

"Do you really think I don't *want* to be with her?" I asked in a desperate voice.

"I have no doubt you do," he answered calmly. "You look like you've been dragged through hell and back. You stayed with her and made sure she was healthy before you dumped her—"

"I didn't dump her," I protested in a surly tone.

"Read her blog post," he suggested. "She thinks you dumped her."

"I did read it. It nearly broke me. If you hadn't come through that door, I probably would have been at her place by now."

"You made her happy, Mason. She loved you. And then you threw everything away because of your own fears. None of this is rational."

"She makes me crazy," I snarled at him. "I don't *feel* rational."

For the first time since the shooting, I had to stop and think about whether Laura really would be safer with me.

Was she better off with me, even if I was an asshole to be with sometimes?

Was any other guy going to be as obsessed with her safety as I was?

Was he going to try to make her happy like she deserved to be?

Was anyone going to love her as obsessively as I did and always would?

Okay, maybe the obsessive part of it wasn't good, but… "No guy will ever love her as much as I do," I confessed to my cousin huskily.

"I don't think it would be possible. I think she really would be safer with me than without me. I would have taken that damn bullet for her in a heartbeat if it would have been possible to it."

"Then you damn well better find a way to make up for the way you've hurt her, because *I'd* like to hurt you for what you've done. I mean, I get the fucked-up logic of trying to protect her, but doing this shit isn't going to make either one of you happy. And Laura deserves to make the call on whether or not she can deal with the way that you love her. Maybe she will, and maybe she won't, but you should have given her that consideration instead of deciding what's best for her unilaterally."

"Why in the hell did you even come here?" I asked irritably.

"Because, like it or not, whether you want to claim me or not, we're family. And I care about Laura. I'd like to see both of you happy," Hudson answered grimly. "I'm surprised your brothers haven't had this discussion with you yet."

"At the moment, neither one of them are speaking to me," I told him somberly. "They think I'm a dick."

Hudson laughed. "I can't say as I blame them."

I glared at him. "I need to think. Get the hell out of my office."

"I'd think fast if I were you."

"Touch her and I will kill you," I told him.

He held up his hands as he stood up. "I'm not backing off as her friend, but I'm not the type of guy who would ever screw with another man's woman. Besides, I haven't found a woman yet who would ever want to take me on."

"I thought you and your brothers were among the most eligible bachelors in the world or something like that," I grunted. "The media stalks all of you most of the time."

He grinned. "You and your brothers have been on those lists, too."

"Yeah," I admitted. "But we're all taken. Have fun with that."

Carter used to get a ton of media attention because he let himself be high-profile as the spokesman for the corporation. But once he was married, the gossip rags had moved on.

"So what are you going to do?" Hudson asked in a more serious tone. "You saw her blog post this morning. I don't care what she said. She still loves you. But she's right. If the effort isn't there on both sides, no matter what, one person can't keep a relationship together. If I hadn't come here today, I have no doubt you would have come to your senses. But your time could be running out to fix this. I think what Laura was trying to say is that she's done lamenting over what she did wrong."

"She didn't do anything wrong," I rumbled.

"So you don't find the scars unattractive?"

I shot him a dirty look. "Hell, no. I hate them because every time I look at them, it reminds me that she suffered. But they also remind me of just how fearless and strong she really is. Shit, she hardly ever complained, even when I knew she was in pain."

Hudson strode toward the door. "I think some groveling might be in order."

"I rarely grovel," I informed him stiffly. Honestly, I couldn't remember when I ever had, but for Laura, I'd do whatever the hell it took for her to give me another shot.

"If you're going to see her today, I won't go there before I leave," Hudson said as he grabbed the door handle to leave.

It was Sunday.

And I didn't plan on letting much more time go by before I saw her again. I couldn't.

"Go home," I demanded.

"Going," Hudson said with a smirk as he exited my office.

I followed him a few minutes later.

Chapter 24

Laura

It was Sunday.

At almost six p.m.

And yes, I *was* in my office.

But I definitely *wasn't* waiting for Mason to call.

Probably because I hadn't heard from him for well over a week now.

The last time I'd seen him was on my birthday. We'd spent the evening together just like I'd explained to Brynn. And then…nothing.

Crickets.

I drummed my fingernails on the desk in my home office, annoyed with myself because I knew that somewhere in my body, there was a sliver of hope that Mason might call and explain exactly why he'd dumped our whole relationship.

I had to wonder when that little piece of anticipation would start to fade every Sunday.

I'd meant what I'd said in my blog post. It was time for me to move on. Sometimes, I just wasn't going to know all the answers, and I wasn't going to have the closure I wanted.

Obviously, I was never going to know exactly why Mason had stopped calling or answering my texts.

I just had to…let it be.

A tear leaked from my eye, and I angrily swept it away.

Mason Lawson didn't deserve another single moment of my sorrow.

I'd done enough mourning of our relationship.

My tear ducts should be as dry as a desert by now since I'd been crying buckets over the last week.

As of today, I was finished wandering around like I was completely empty inside. I was just going to have to find something to fill me up again.

Eventually.

I startled as my phone started blasting a different Taylor Swift tune as my ringtone: "We're Never Ever Getting Back Together."

Not that Mason had actually *tried* to hook up again, but the song was more of a reminder for myself that it wasn't happening.

I picked up my cell, and gaped as I saw who was calling.

Mason?

Rather than relief, I felt nothing but anger.

Why in the hell was he calling me now?

Curiosity got the better of me, though. "Hello?"

"Can you buzz me in?" he asked brusquely, with no other prelude.

I hesitated. "You're here?"

"Yes. I left something here. Can you let me in?"

My irritation flared. "You're just going to show up, on a Sunday, at six p.m., and tell me you want to come up to my apartment after you haven't answered a single one of my texts or my calls for over a week? Are you crazy?"

"As a matter of fact, yes," he said calmly. "Just let me come up for a minute."

"No." I said firmly, and probably a little bit rudely.

"Yes."

"No."

"Please."

Oh, God. When did Mason ever say please?

That one little word made me melt.

I felt my resolve slip just a little. "Whatever it is that you left, I'll send it to you," I offered shortly.

Mason didn't really bring anything with him when he visited me at my place, and I hadn't come across anything of his that he'd left.

"You can't send it to me," he said obstinately. "I have to pick it up personally. It's important."

Fine. I want answers, right? I want closure. Here's my chance. If he wants this unknown item back, he's going to have to answer my questions first.

I got up and buzzed him in, allowing him to step through the secured front door of the condo complex.

I leaned against the wall near my front door as I waited for him to come up. "I can do this. I'll get my answers, and he'll get whatever the hell he left here. I can do this. I can do this."

I couldn't stop whispering my mantra, even though it wasn't really helping.

Maybe I really needed to see the cool, disinterested Mason to finally close the door entirely on our relationship.

Maybe I needed to see him for who he really was.

God, I needed *something,* because I was far from being over him, no matter what I'd posted on my blog.

In theory, what I'd said in my blog was exactly what I wanted to do.

But my damn heart couldn't stop warring with my common sense.

In fact, my heart was racing so fast that I was starting to feel dizzy.

I stood up straight when my doorbell rang, stiffening my spine to deal with the encounter.

I can do this! I can do this!

I opened the door, and the moment I saw him, I nearly gave in to the urge to fling myself into his arms.

It was a Sunday, so he was dressed casually in a pair of jeans and a blue polo shirt.

He looked exhausted.

He looked like he had lost weight.

His eyes weren't cool and elusive as I'd expected.

They were dark and filled with turmoil.

He looked…tormented.

I silently opened the door wider to let him in, and then closed it behind him.

I can do this! I can do this!

"Before I give you whatever you left here, I'd just like a few answers to my questions," I said in a cool voice. "You're not going to grab whatever you want and go."

He moved toward the living room, and I followed him.

"Can we sit?" he asked. "Please. I'll answer any questions you have, and I want to say something if you'll let me. I can't grab what I want. Not right now."

If I'd expected him to defensive, I was all wrong.

He sat in a recliner, and I was so antsy that I perched on the arm of my couch. "What did you leave here?" I questioned abruptly.

He looked up at me with those fevered gray eyes of his, and simply said, "My heart."

My eyes widened as I looked at him suspiciously. "What?"

"I said, I left my heart here. With you, Laura. It's been yours pretty much from the first time I saw you."

Oh, shit. Maybe I *couldn't* do this.

The low, solemn tone of his voice sent a shiver down my spine. "*You* dumped *me*," I reminded him in a heated tone. I wasn't about to just crumble because of his sweet declaration. He *had* stop talking to me for over a week.

"I didn't *dump* you, Laura. I was terrified." He stood up again, and started pacing around the room like a caged tiger. "When you got shot, I lost my shit completely. I thought the only way to keep you safe was to push you away from me. You shouldn't have been at that restaurant. You wouldn't have been if my cousin hadn't lured you there on a pretense. What happens the next time something happens because of me? What if a business nemesis pops up and tries to hurt you or kill you to get revenge on me? Or they kidnap you? *Christ!* Now that I say that, I'm still not sure if I'm doing the right thing by begging you to give me another shot. But I can't *not* be your guy, either, because I know damn well no other man is ever going to love you as much as I do."

My heart tripped as I watched him continue to move around the living room.

Once I caught my breath, I asked, "So you didn't return my calls because you didn't want me to be associated with you?"

"Yes. I thought you'd be safer away from me. Not that you were ever actually alone. My guys have been keeping an eye on you."

"They have?" I said, surprised.

"Of course."

He said that like I should have known that he'd keep his security on my ass. I hadn't noticed them, so he'd obviously done it pretty covertly.

"You love me?" I said quietly, not quite sure what to say. "I told you I loved you, but you never said it back."

"I wanted to," he said fiercely. "You have no idea how badly I wanted to tell you, too. But if I had, I never would have been able to let you go. Hell, I can't now, and you haven't said it again."

"Could you stop for a minute? You're making me dizzy, Mason." I stepped in front of him on his next pass. He collided with my body, but grabbed me fast enough to keep me from harm.

"Damn it. Don't do that," he said in a ragged voice. "I could have run you over."

"I want you to just talk to me," I said softly.

He took me by the shoulders and looked at me like a man who was being tortured. "Here's the biggest problem, Laura...I love you too damn much. I love you like a madman. I can't stand the thought of anything happening to you. You almost died because of me."

I took a deep breath and let it out slowly, trying to absorb exactly what he was telling me.

He'd pushed me away because he was afraid I'd get hurt again.

He was *obsessed* over not letting it happen again.

He blamed himself for what had happened. *That one* bothered me the most. "What happened wasn't your fault, Mason. Yes, I took an appointment with Hudson, but who's to say I wouldn't have been there eating anyway. I was just in the wrong place at the wrong time."

I could see the guilt etched into his face, and my anger fell away. He'd obviously been tormenting himself about this long enough.

He shook his head. "Nice try, but you were, in fact, there because of me."

God, he was so stubborn. "It's not going to happen again."

"How can I know that?" he asked in a strained voice.

"You can't. Not completely. None of us are fortune tellers. But I would have chosen to be with you no matter what. You didn't choose me."

"I thought I did," he said huskily. "I thought I was putting you first. Would you ever really want to be with a guy who obsesses over your safety all the damn time?"

I had to bite back a smile. "You always have. It would have taken compromise, understanding, and time, especially considering what happened. But you chose to just push me away instead. You hurt me, Mason. You didn't talk to me about it. You just made a decision that I'd be better off without you."

"Not on purpose. Never on purpose," he vowed hoarsely.

I let out a shaky breath. "I think I know that now. But I don't think you realize that I need you to be with me. I need to know that you aren't going to run away when things get difficult."

"I fucked up," he confessed. "But I'd never abandon you. Never again. You said you were moving on. I can't. There's never going to be anyone else for me, Laura. You're it. And that's pretty damn scary."

Now that I understood Mason's motivation, I knew I could deal with it. The memory of what had happened was fresh in his at the moment, but it would fade away in time. Problem was, I'd never known about how badly he feared something happening to me again because he hadn't talked to me about it.

Honestly, if our roles had been reversed, I probably would have felt the same way. I would have wanted to cling to him, at least for a while, to reassure myself that he wasn't going to scare the hell out of me like that again.

"We could have worked through both of our fears together, Mason."

"Tell me that we still can, Laura," he said stubbornly.

"Right now, I don't know what to say," I told him as I moved to sit back on the arm of the couch before my legs gave out. "A few minutes ago, I thought you dumped me because you lost interest. You saw me at my weakest, my ugliest, and I assumed I wasn't what you wanted."

He moved in front of me and stroked a hand over my hair gently. "You could never be weak or ugly to me. You're the strongest woman I know. I read your blog. Did you really think your scars could be anything except proof of your strength to me?"

A river of tears started to flow, and I let them. "I didn't know. You shut me out. You wouldn't even really kiss me."

"If I had, I never would have let you go, sweetheart," he rumbled. "I love you too damn much."

"Stop saying that," I said angrily as I punched him in the shoulder. "You could never love me too much. Dammit, Mason. Don't you understand that I love you the same way? I love you so much that—"

I never got another word out of my mouth because he had me up, cradled in his arms, and thoroughly silenced me as his lips crushed mine in less than a heartbeat.

Chapter 25

Laura

I shuddered as Mason tightened his arms around me, and kissed me like he couldn't survive without my mouth.

I wrapped my arms around his neck, relishing the groan that appeared to be torn from him as it vibrated against my lips.

This was what I'd wanted.

This was what I'd needed.

This is what I'd craved.

I love you too damn much.

That's what he'd said, but he didn't understand that this kind of passion from him was what I yearned for with him.

I could handle the crazy way he loved me, because I loved *him* in exactly the same way.

What I *couldn't* deal with was him emotionally running away. When he'd shut me out, and blew me off, it had devastated me.

We were both huffing to catch our breath when he finally lifted his head.

"I'm sorry," he panted as he put his forehead on mine. "I didn't mean to do that. I couldn't stop."

I looked up at him. "I missed you. I missed this," I said, my voice trembling with emotion. "It's been so long since you've kissed me like that."

"I love you, Laura," he said in a graveled voice. "I should have said it before, and I never should have let you think otherwise. But sometimes I don't know how to handle…us."

"You're going to have to learn if we're going to try this again. I can't do this again if we aren't in it together," I warned him.

"I'm all in," he promised. "Are you going to give me another shot?"

I nodded slowly. "I suppose I am, because I love you too much to give up."

"Thank fuck!" he answered, sounding immensely relieved.

"Just don't mess with my insecurities again," I teased him.

"Like I've said before, you have nothing to be insecure about," he growled. "Do you really think I give a damn about what you look like, or how your scars look?"

"When you don't talk to me, my mind is always going to go to the worst scenario," I told him honestly. "What else would I think? How was I supposed to know that you were trying to protect me?"

"Then I'll fucking talk until you're sick of listening to me."

I snorted. "That would be a change."

Somehow, I couldn't imagine Mason suddenly starting to babble on about his every emotion. He wouldn't. But I had to trust he'd do the best he could.

"I love you," I told him firmly. "I'm putting my emotional sanity into your hands because I don't want to let you go."

"You'll never regret it," he answered, like he was making a vow. "Now let me take a good look at those scars."

I rapped him on the shoulder. "What? You think you're just going to waltz in here, take off my clothes, and take me to bed?"

Honestly, the only thing I wanted to do was to get him naked, but I wasn't willing to let him out of hot water that easily.

"Not happening?" he said, sounding disappointed. "No problem. I'm willing to wait for you. I'll always wait for you. You can let me know when you're ready. Until then, we'll just talk. Be friends. Everything is on your terms right now, baby."

When I looked into his beautiful gray eyes, I melted. Mason wasn't going to push me. I could see that he was too afraid that I'd change my mind.

He'll do anything I want. Even if that means suffering through a bad case of blue balls until I say the word.

I put my lips against his ear and whispered, "You're not taking my clothes off because I'd much rather undress you."

"Oh, fuck me. You'll kill me," he groaned.

I reached for the bottom of his shirt. "I plan on fucking you, big guy," I said, feeling like the sexiest woman in the world at the moment. "But I'm getting you naked first."

He lifted his arms, his eyes flashing with fire.

I pulled off the shirt and tossed it aside. He stood perfectly still as I put my hands on his chest and touched every inch of bare skin I could find.

God, he felt so good.

Mason had always felt amazing.

Every muscle was tense, and I could tell he was like a powder keg ready to blow. I marveled at his control as my hands went lower, savoring every inch of his rock-hard abs until I was finally tracing that enticing trail of hair that disappeared into the waistband of his low-slung jeans.

"Are you trying to punish me?" he asked hoarsely.

I flipped the button on his pants. "Maybe just a little," I confessed.

"Fine. I can take it," he said, not sounding at all comfortable, no matter what he said.

I copped a feel of his enormous erection with my palm. "You're so hard, Mason," I crooned.

God, I loved the way he wanted me. I'd missed it so much.

I wanted the craziness.

I wanted the insanity.

I wanted the desperation we always felt to be together.

It was a mad love, but I wouldn't want it any other way.

I struggled to get the zipper down around his enormous cock, but I finally freed him and tugged the jeans down his legs, along with his boxer briefs. He kicked them off like he was happy they were gone.

I took a long breath and inhaled his masculine, unique scent. Mason smelled like…Mason.

Earthy.

Wild.

Uninhibited.

Carnal.

Intense.

Sexy.

And completely delicious.

"You have to be the most beautifully made man I've ever seen," I told him honestly.

He visibly swallowed, like he was actually nervous. "I'm thick," he grumbled, repeating the words I'd once said to him.

I smiled at him. "Then I guess thick men get me very wet. You look pretty damn hot to me." I gave him an answer similar to the one he'd given me as I wrapped my fingers around his cock.

"Don't," he warned me huskily. "It won't take much to make me come."

I used my thumb to spread the drop of moisture at his tip around the silky head. "And that's a problem? Why?"

The keg finally exploded. Mason sprang forward, buried his hands in my hair, and took control.

I breathed a contented sigh against his lips as he kissed me like he couldn't wait another second for our bodies to somehow be connected. I felt the buttons on the blouse I was wearing pop as he stripped it open and started to drag it down my arms.

"I need to fucking touch you," he said as his mouth left mine.

"Damn. I was so enjoying the view," I said in a passionate, husky tone.

"My turn," he demanded as he unclasped my bra from the front catch, and my breasts flowed into his hands. "*Jesus!* I feel like I've waited forever to touch these beauties again."

I let the bra fall down and off while Mason teased the hard nipples, and then swooped down to torment each one of them with his mouth.

"Mason," I moaned as I closed my eyes and got lost in the sensation of this man I adored worshipping my body. "Fuck me."

"Not yet," he growled as his tongue rolled over the scars left from my surgery, and the multitude of other procedures that had needed to be done to save my life.

I opened my eyes, and tears flowed freely. Without words, I knew what Mason was trying to say: there wasn't a single thing about my body that he didn't love.

"I love you so much. Too much," I moaned.

"Never too much," he grunted as he dropped to his knees and pulled the flowy skirt I was wearing down my legs, dragging my panties off with it.

I literally screamed as he leaned forward and buried his face into my pussy, laving and sucking like his life depended on thoroughly tasting me.

"Mason, please," I whimpered. I needed him inside me.

"Please what? Please do this?" he asked gruffly right before he found my clit and flicked his tongue over the swollen bud.

"Oh, God," I muttered desperately, knowing that I'd be begging him to make me come in another few seconds.

He didn't tease, and he didn't mess around. Mason was on a mission, and his objective was to have me screaming his name as I climaxed without a single inhibition left in my body.

I speared my hands into his dark hair, urging him on as I spread my legs to give him better access.

He purred approvingly like a big cat, sending pulsations through my entire body.

"Yes. Oh, God. Mason!" I screamed because I couldn't help myself. "I-can't-take-anymore-you're-killing-me-please-please-please!"

He plunged his fingers inside me, using them to fuck me, and my body exploded like a stick of dynamite. My orgasm shook me to my core, and Mason's tongue was there to lap up every drop, extending the pleasure until I felt like I was raw and vulnerable.

I panted as I came back to Earth, my body damp with perspiration.

I kept my hand in his hair as he rose to his feet, and I tugged slightly as I demanded, "Fuck me. Now."

I wanted this man so deep inside me that I felt like we were permanently joined.

He kissed me, letting me taste myself on his lips, before he said roughly, "Have to. I can't wait anymore."

I shivered with anticipation as he drew me to the back of the couch, placed my hands on it, and said, "Hold on."

Mason had never taken me from behind. He'd always been too afraid the position would be too deep.

"Yes," I hissed, eager for him to do it before he changed his mind.

Groans of satisfaction left both of our mouths in tandem as he buried himself to the hilt inside me, his hands gripped tightly on my hips to hold me steady.

I lowered my head, the pleasure of being completely by taken by Mason almost too much to handle.

I felt his hesitation as he said, "Too much?"

"No! For God's sake, don't stop!" I pleaded. "I need you like this."

Hard and hot.

Rough and raw.

Every single inch of him.

I craved him, and I needed both of us to be satisfied after being apart for so long.

He drew back, and surged inside me again. "I'll never give you a reason to doubt me again," he growled as he started a deep, rapid rhythm that had my body thrumming with desperate need. "You're mine, Laura. You have been since the moment you let me take you the first time."

"Yes," I whimpered, my body on fire because alpha Mason was back with a vengeance.

And I loved every bossy, demanding, overbearing part of him.

I could put him in his place when I had to, but right at the moment, I just wanted to be...his.

"Harder," I demanded.

He gave me harder, our skin slapping together the most erotic thing I'd ever heard.

"You're so damn wet. So damn tight," he grunted. "I can't wait much longer."

"Don't," I insisted.

But I should have known better. He'd never come until I did.

Mason snaked his hand around my body and buried his fingers in my pussy, caressing my clit with strong fingers that knew exactly what they were doing.

I imploded, my entire body shaking as I screamed his name at the height of my pleasure. "Mason, I love you!"

"I love you, too, baby," he groaned as my body milked him to his own release.

An animalistic sound left his lips as he gripped my hips tightly and let go, and I savored it.

That was Mason.

Losing control.

Over…me.

Just as my legs were about to give out, he caught me in his arms and carried me to the couch. He flopped onto the leather fabric, taking me down with him, my sated body sagging on top of him.

We were both hot, sweaty, and completely satisfied.

He wrapped his arms protectively around my body, and muttered incomprehensible words into my hair as he held me.

"You can never love me too damn much." He finally said something I could comprehend. "Love me, Laura. Love me as much as you can."

I nuzzled my face into his neck. "I already do," I told him tenderly. "And don't worry about loving me too much. I need you, Mason. I can handle whatever you throw my way."

"Just remember you said that," he grumbled.

I smiled against his salty skin, knowing that whatever happened, we'd always manage to work it out now.

No matter how different we were, Mason and I just…fit.

We were supposed to be together.

My heart told me that we were exactly where we were supposed to be.

As he'd once said to me: *everything else will just work itself out.*

Epilogue

Laura

"Marry me, and just put me out of my misery," Mason grumbled a few months later as he presented me with the most beautiful diamond ring I'd ever seen.

He'd taken me to one of the fancy ball fundraisers that he hated, but insisted they weren't *all that bad* anymore because I was there with him.

When we'd gotten home, he'd pulled a red velvet box from his pocket while I was sitting on his sofa, taking off my heels.

He was on his knees right beside me, the expression on his face tormented.

I'd recently agreed to live with him in his beautiful home. I'd sold my condo, which had been a huge commitment, and while it hadn't been easy working everything out between us, I loved him just as fiercely as I had when we'd gotten back together.

Slowly, we'd found a way to meet somewhere in the middle. Maybe I *had* given a little bit more in the beginning, when all of Mason's fears were still fresh in his mind. But he'd relaxed after a couple of weeks, and we'd eventually been able to meet in the middle.

I understood his fears.

He understood my need to have some privacy.

To have the kind of unconditional love Mason showed me on a daily basis, soothing his fears hadn't been all that difficult.

Sure, I knew that we'd probably always have our squabbles.

Mason would get too high-handed.

And I'd finally put my foot down.

However, I'd learned that we'd *always* do it with love.

My eyes met his, and I could see that he was actually…nervous.

He was letting himself be vulnerable right now, and his openness touched my heart.

Not once had Mason even tried to run away from a conflict.

He stayed and worked it out. Every. Single. Time.

I reached out and touched the diamond gingerly. The center diamond was enormous, but it looked flawless. I loved the tiny bunches of smaller diamonds around it, making it appear to be the shape of a flower. "It's beautiful. And so unique."

"Just like you," he drawled, which made me smile.

I loved the way that Mason had alleviated every single fear I'd had about him walking away again.

He'd been sincere when he'd said I'd never have reason to doubt him again.

He spoiled me unabashedly, and freely talked to me when he had something on his mind.

If he started feeling crazy protective, we'd talk about that, too, and I'd tried to find different ways to distract him. Generally, hot sex worked the best.

"Say yes," he said impatiently. "Jesus! I hate myself for every time I gave my brothers hell about needing to marry their wives. I'm just as damn pathetic as they were."

I chuckled before I said, "You already know I'm going to say *yes*."

"I don't," he argued. "Which is why I'm still here in a tuxedo on bended knee."

I reached out and stroked my palm along the dark shadow on his jawline. "Yes. I love you, Mason. I want to be your wife."

He yanked the ring out of the box and tossed it aside. "Thank fuck!" he said with what sounded like relief as he slipped the ring on my finger. "I love you, too, Laura. I always will."

I leaned forward and gave him a tender kiss on the lips, and he didn't push it into anything further. He just kissed me over and over, with a gentleness that touched me so much that I started to cry.

Finally, he pulled back and sat on the couch beside me. "Don't cry," he insisted. "I really hate it when you cry."

I'd discovered that there was nothing Mason dreaded more than to see me in tears. "It's a happy cry," I said with a sniffle.

He shrugged out of his jacket, and then pulled me into his lap.

I sighed as I put my head on his shoulder. I'd given up on insisting I was too heavy to sit on his lap a long time ago because he liked having me there.

Truthfully, I relished being this close to Mason, too.

Because Mason treated me like the sexiest woman on Earth, I'd lost almost every insecurity I'd ever had about my height, weight, and my body overall.

There had been plenty of hot, steamy nights when he'd made me love the way we fit together so perfectly.

"I guess I've never really understood the benefit of crying when you're actually happy, but I'll have to take your word on that," he said, sounding as content as I'd ever heard him. "No reservations?"

"Not a single one. You've been a man of your word," I teased.

"Can we set the date soon?" he asked pensively.

"Whenever you want," I answered agreeably.

"Tomorrow," he replied, sounding completely serious.

"Not quite *that* soon," I objected. "Planning a wedding takes time. It doesn't have to be a huge wedding. But I'd like all of your family to be there."

"I do, too," he admitted reluctantly.

"Are you going to invite your cousins?" I knew that Mason and Hudson had gotten closer. Mason hadn't had much of a choice since his cousin had been persistent, and Hudson was still a good friend to me.

"That would mean I'd have to tell my siblings the truth," he mused.

"Yes," I agreed.

"I think I'm ready to do it now," he said with a certainty I'd never heard from him before about this particular subject.

"No pressure," I reminded him. "If you never feel like you want to tell them, that's up to you."

"I really don't think it's going to make a difference. You were right. I do need to see it for myself, even though I already know it won't matter."

My heart skittered as I said, "Are you sure?"

He nodded. "I am. It's time. They're my siblings, and since I met you, you've convinced me that I'm not *different*. I am a Lawson, through and through. I always will be."

Thank God!

Although I would have supported Mason in whatever decision he made, I was glad that he'd finally know for sure that his family didn't give a damn if he only had half their DNA.

"Oh, you're a Lawson all right," I said with a smile. "You're just as stubborn as your siblings."

He grinned. "And just as obsessive about my woman as my brothers."

Honestly, Mason *was* getting better. He'd been much more relaxed the last few weeks. As time passed, his anxiety decreased. Not that I believed that there would ever come a time when he didn't take my well-being seriously, but I could handle that. I understood it. If I had seen Mason in a hospital bed badly injured, I'd be freaked about his safety for a long time, too.

Mason was silent for a few minutes before he said, "We're only getting married once. I want you to have the wedding of your dreams."

I stroked a hand over the nape of his neck. "I have the *groom* of my dreams. That's enough for me."

What did it matter *how* it happened? All I cared about was having the *right man*.

Mason was the one guy I thought I'd never have.

He'd been unattainable…until he wasn't anymore.

He was the man who loved me exactly the way I was, and he'd changed my life forever with that love.

"I'm probably not the Prince Charming you were always looking for," he said drily.

No, he wasn't. "You're not," I agreed. "You're so much more."

His grin grew larger. "So you'd be willing to let me be your baby daddy?"

I nodded. "I'm hoping you will. I think I'd like to have our child. And if you're willing, we could adopt from the system, too. My business is doing well, and I think I could slow it down, and take some time to just be a wife and a mother for a while."

I held my breath as I watched Mason swallow nervously. "That means you'd have to go through pregnancy. And labor."

I released the air I'd been holding. He wasn't unwilling. He just didn't want to watch me go through pregnancy and the pain of labor. "You'd be there with me. I'd be fine."

"I'm not sure I will be," he told me grimly. "But I won't pretend like I wouldn't love to see you get that child you always wanted."

"I still want it," I admitted. "But I don't *need* it anymore."

I had Mason, and any children we might adopt in the future. That was more than enough.

"I want it, too."

I lifted my head and looked into his eyes. The sincerity in his expression made my heart skip a beat. "You really do?"

He nodded. "I really do."

"I'm thirty-five now. You'll have some work to do in the near future."

"I think I'm up to it."

I squirmed as I felt the proof of that statement beneath my rear end. "I know you are," I teased.

He took my head gently between his hands, prompting me to look at him as he said, "I love you, Laura. With or without us having our own children. It's your call, sweetheart."

My heart contracted so hard that I could hardly breathe. How did I ever get lucky enough to have a future husband like Mason? "Even if I end my birth control, there's no guarantee it will happen."

He shrugged, the wicked grin on his face deliciously mischievous as he said huskily, "Then we'll have one hell of a good time trying."

I laughed as I wrapped my arms around his neck. "I think I'd be more than happy just to leave it up to fate at this point. I don't think I could be happier than I am right now. With you."

Two years ago, I'd thought that all I'd *wanted* was to have a child.

Now, I knew better.

What I'd really *needed* was Mason.

"No reason we can't start practicing right now," Mason said in a wicked, wicked voice.

I smiled as I lowered my head to kiss the man I loved more than anything or anyone else in the world.

I wasn't about to argue with him about honing our skills at baby-making, whether it resulted in us having a child…or not.

What I'd told him before was still true today. Maybe it was ever truer now than it had been the last time I'd thought about it.

I wanted to have our child, but I didn't *need* it.

Once, I'd mistakenly believed that having a kid was everything I wanted.

I'd been so wrong.

What I'd really needed was a man who would accept me exactly the way I was, and not want to change me.

Somebody to love me unconditionally.

Somebody to make me feel special, sexy, and completely and utterly loved.

I'd found that in the man right in front of me.

"Would you be horribly disappointed if I can't conceive?" I asked him softly.

He shook his head immediately, and put his hand behind my head, his eyes laser-focused on mine. "Hell, no. We can still adopt, and I have you, Laura. Knowing you're mine is more than enough for me."

I sent him a tremulous smile. Every time Mason said something like that, I realized just how lucky I was that I'd found him.

I'll never have to kiss another frog.

Mason was, after all, my Prince Charming, and he was more than enough for me, too.

~The End~

Be sure to pre-order the next book in The Billionaire's Obsession series, Billionaire Undercover, Hudson Montgomery's story.

Author Acknowledgments

There are always so many people to thank in the back of a book, because there are so many whose effort makes my book come to life.

Many thanks to my personal team, Dani, Natalie, Isa, and Annette for the energy you put into making each book a successful new release.

I couldn't do what I do without an amazing husband who almost always ends up on his own with the cooking and taking care of other household tasks while I write like a maniac.

I'm grateful for my reader group/street team, Jan's Gems for every single you do to support my books.

Last, but not least, I'm incredibly grateful to my readers. It's all of you who allow me to keep doing what I love to do, and make a living out of it. Thank you all for your continued, enthusiastic support for my billionaire's.

Xoxoxoxoxo - Jan

Please visit me at:
http://www.authorjsscott.com
http://www.facebook.com/authorjsscott

You can write to me at
jsscott_author@hotmail.com

You can also tweet
@AuthorJSScott

Please sign up for my Newsletter for updates, new releases and exclusive excerpts.

Books by J. S. Scott:

Billionaire Obsession Series

The Billionaire's Obsession~Simon
Heart of the Billionaire
The Billionaire's Salvation
The Billionaire's Game
Billionaire Undone~Travis
Billionaire Unmasked~Jason
Mine for Christmas (Simon and Kara Short Novella)
Billionaire Untamed~Tate
Billionaire Unbound~Chloe
Billionaire Undaunted~Zane
Billionaire Unknown~Blake
Billionaire Unveiled~Marcus
Billionaire Unloved~Jett

Billionaire Unchallenged~Carter
Billionaire Unattainable~Mason

Sinclair Series

The Billionaire's Christmas
No Ordinary Billionaire
The Forbidden Billionaire
The Billionaire's Touch
The Billionaire's Voice
The Billionaire Takes All
The Billionaire's Secret
Only A Millionaire

Accidental Billionaires

Ensnared
Entangled
Enamored (October 15, 2019)

Walker Brothers Series

Release
Player
Damaged

The Sentinel Demons

The Sentinel Demons: The Complete Collection
A Dangerous Bargain
A Dangerous Hunger
A Dangerous Fury
A Dangerous Demon King

The Vampire Coalition Series

The Vampire Coalition: The Complete Collection
The Rough Mating of a Vampire (Prelude)
Ethan's Mate
Rory's Mate
Nathan's Mate
Liam's Mate
Daric's Mate

Changeling Encounters Series

Changeling Encounters: The Complete Collection
Mate Of The Werewolf
The Dangers Of Adopting A Werewolf
All I Want For Christmas Is A Werewolf

The Pleasures of His Punishment

The Pleasures of His Punishment: The Complete Collection
The Billionaire Next Door
The Millionaire and the Librarian
Riding with the Cop
Secret Desires of the Counselor
In Trouble with the Boss
Rough Ride with a Cowboy
Rough Day for the Teacher
A Forfeit for a Cowboy
Just what the Doctor Ordered
Wicked Romance of a Vampire

The Curve Collection: Big Girls and Bad Boys Series

The Curve Collection: The Complete Collection

The Curve Ball

The Beast Loves Curves

Curves by Design

Writing as Lane Parker

Dearest Stalker: Part 1

Dearest Stalker: A Complete Collection

A Christmas Dream

A Valentine's Dream

Lost: A Mountain Man Rescue Romance

A Dark Horse Novel w/ Cali MacKay

Bound

Hacked

Taken By A Trillionaire Series

Virgin for the Trillionaire by Ruth Cardello

Virgin for the Prince by J.S. Scott

Virgin to Conquer by Melody Anne

Prince Bryan: Taken By A Trillionaire

Left at the Altar Series

Temporary Groom (Book 1)

Other Titles

Well Played w/Ruth Cardello

57636659R00128

Made in the USA
Middletown, DE
01 August 2019